'Tis the Time, 'Tis the Season

Endorsements

Chris Posti does a fantastic job weaving the struggles of faith, family, and friendships through heartache, loss, and success. Her three main characters are far from perfect. Marla, Suzanne, and Rachel, united by high school memories and relationships, find their friendships and faith challenged in coming home to face unexpected changes. The surprising turns and engaging characters will keep you turning pages until the satisfying and unforeseen ending.
—**Donna K. Stearns**, author of *The Nazarene's Price* and *Cost and Crown*

In this novel penned by Chris Posti, we learn that life and love know no age limits, as her characters traverse the trials of wit versus selflessness. Posti's words portray the witty and entertaining dynamics between three best friends as they navigate this coming of age filled with romance aplenty.
—**Claire O'Sullivan**, author of the Whiskey River Mystery series: *Romance Under Wraps–book 1, Silk & Slippers–book 2,* and *Rules of Engagement*, a thriller;

Chris Posti has written an intriguing sequel to her second book in this series. The reader will enjoy reacquainting themselves with three former high school friends, who are now approaching their senior years. This book has enough drama and hope to keep women's fiction readers turning pages in this satisfying read.
—**Bettie Boswell**, author of Christian romance, suspense, and children's books

'Tis the Time, 'Tis the Season

CHRIS POSTI

A Christian Company
ElkLakePublishingInc.com

Copyright Notice

'Tis the Time, 'Tis the Season
First edition. Copyright © 2024 by Chris Posti. The information contained in this book is the intellectual property of Chris Posti and is governed by United States and International copyright laws. All rights reserved. No part of this publication, either text or image, may be used for any purpose other than personal use. Therefore, reproduction, modification, storage in a retrieval system, or retransmission, in any form or by any means, electronic, mechanical, or otherwise, for reasons other than personal use, except for brief quotations for reviews or articles and promotions, is strictly prohibited without prior written permission by the publisher.

NO AI TRAINING: Without in any way limiting Chris Posti's and publisher's exclusive rights under copyright, any use of this publication to "train" generative artificial intelligence (AI) technologies to generate text is expressly prohibited. The author reserves all rights to license uses of this work for generative AI training and development of machine learning language models.

This is a work of fiction. Names, characters, businesses, places, events, locales, and incidents are either the products of the author's imagination or used in a fictitious manner. Any resemblance to actual persons, living or dead, or actual events is purely coincidental.

Scripture Version: Scriptures marked NIV are taken from the NEW INTERNATIONAL VERSION (NIV): Scriptures taken from THE HOLY BIBLE, NEW INTERNATIONAL VERSION ®. Copyright©1973, 1978, 1984, 2011 by Biblica, Inc.™. Used by permission of Zondervan.

Cover and Interior Design: Kelly Artieri, Deb Haggerty
Editor(s): Cristel Phelps, Deb Haggerty

PUBLISHED BY: Elk Lake Publishing, Inc., 35 Dogwood Drive, Plymouth, MA 02360, 2024

Library Cataloging Data

Names: Posti, Chris (Chris Posti)

'Tis the Time, 'Tis the Season / Chris, Posti

312 p. 23cm × 15cm (9in × 6 in.)

ISBN-13: 9798891342651 (paperback) | 9798891342668 (trade paperback) | 9798891342675 (ebook)

Key Words: Christian Romance Books for Adults; Uplifting Christian Fiction; Romance Novels for Older Women; Small Town Romance Books; Second Chance Romance Books; Novels for Older Women; Novels about Older Women

Library of Congress Control Number: 2024947288 Fiction

Dedication

To my grandsons, Christian and Nathan,
who light up my life like nobody else.

Acknowledgments

My sincere thanks to the staff at Auberle (https://www.auberle.org/) in Western Pennsylvania and New Life Village (https://newlifevillage.org/) in Tampa, Florida. These amazing organizations inspired the plot of this novel. My hope is readers will be moved to pray for them, provide financial support, become a foster or adoptive parent, volunteer their time and talents—and even replicate what Marla creates in this story.

My thanks also go to Charles J. Carlini and Gail Mazzei for sharing their valuable medical expertise.

I am so grateful for publisher Deb Haggerty of Elk Lake Publishing and editor Cristel Phelps, who have ushered me through this series of three novels. They have been generous with both advice and patience. My thanks also goes to graphic designer, Kelly Artieri, new to this series.

What a miracle that the Lord brought Kristine Delano, Diane Samson, and Jamie Ogle into my life. Faithful critique partners for all three novels, they have become my treasured sisters in Christ.

Above all, I thank my Heavenly Father, who has blessed me with every word of this novel. Apart from Him, I can do nothing.

Chapter 1

MARLA

As the sun dipped beneath the horizon, casting its final fiery glow across the snow-covered western Pennsylvania landscape, Marla Galani emerged from the sleek confines of a limousine. With practiced ease, she flicked her wrist and handed the driver a crisp fifty.

Her long mane of dark hair swirled in the brisk wind as she made her way along the shoveled path to Hope Hospital. The entrance doors glided apart, and she stepped inside. Despite the whoosh of warm air, she couldn't shake off the chill that seemed to linger. In front of her stood an inflated Santa and oversized nutcrackers, garish decorations that seemed out of place. If this was the hospital's way of distracting people from their suffering, it hadn't worked on Marla.

She followed a swath of plastic candy canes to the registration desk. "I'm here to see Grace Symanski—I mean Walton."

The guard sized her up with a prolonged squint.

"She just got married. That's her new last name. I'm her ... her mother." *Walton. Mother.* Would those words ever come to her lips naturally?

"You got ID?"

Marla dug her driver's license from her soft leather bag and handed it to him.

"New York?" The guard looked her over. "Here in Port Mariette, we don't get many visitors from out of state." He handed her license back. "Room 311. Elevators are over there on the right." An unnecessary direction, at least for Marla. It had been more than forty years since her aunt secreted her in here, yet there are some things you never forget.

On the third floor, Marla made a beeline for the busy nurses' station. "Can you tell me where Grace Walton is? I'm her mother." This time, it came out more naturally. Practice, practice, practice.

One of the nurses looked up from her computer screen.

Marla gave her a smile, in the hope it would generate a helpful response. "How's Grace doing?"

"She's fine." A phone rang, and the nurse dismissed Marla with a pointed finger. "Her room's that way. I'll stop by in a few minutes."

Marla hurried down the hall, wondering what *fine* would look like on her daughter.

Peeking inside the room, she spotted Grace, eyes closed, lying in bed, and Jesse, her husband of only three months, holding her hand, his head bowed over her blanketed body.

Love so palpable, her heart ached to witness it.

"May I come in?" Marla whispered it loud enough for them to react, but she flew into the room before either of them answered.

"Marla." Grace's dark eyes flashed open then bounced back and forth between Marla and Jesse.

He looked at Grace and winced. "I ... I called her when the doctor was asking about your family medical history. In all the rush, I forgot to mention it to you."

"It's okay, Jesse." Grace squeezed his hand. "Why don't you go get a bite to eat? You must be starving."

He shot out of the room, the grimace still etched on his face.

Newlyweds. They were still figuring each other out.

Marla slipped off her silk-lined cashmere coat and took a seat in the chair Jesse had vacated. "You weren't expecting me?" She may not have been invited, but she had a right to be here.

Grace pulled the blanket over her shoulder. "I didn't want anybody to know. Other than Jesse, of course."

"I won't tell anyone. I promise."

"Not Warren, not Suzanne. Not even Aunt Sissy," Grace said, "and I really mean that."

"You're not going to tell your only aunt? Don't you think Rachel ought to know?"

"A ruptured ectopic pregnancy at age forty-two? Not the kind of news I'd like to share. All those questions. All that syrupy sympathy. No thanks."

"Got it. Mum's the word." Not telling Warren would be easy. But how would she keep such a secret from her girlfriends? Back in high school, Rachel—aka Aunt Sissy—and Suzanne had been Marla's best friends, and after their fortieth reunion here last July, they'd bonded anew.

Marla rested a hand on her daughter's arm. "I'm so sorry this happened, Grace," she whispered. "So sorry." She didn't know what else to say. Words of comfort didn't come easily.

"Thank you." Grace blinked a few times then pursed her lips. "Let's not talk about it right now, okay? Too painful."

Marla leaned back on the cracked vinyl armrest, staying silent for only a moment. "I can't believe they didn't put you in an ambulance and get you to one of the hospitals up in Pittsburgh. Couldn't they have driven you a half-hour north?"

"There wasn't time. I was bleeding too much."

Marla tapped her red nails on the armrests. "Well, under those circumstances, I guess bringing you here made sense, but they should have taken care of it laparoscopically instead of butchering you with a scalpel."

"They couldn't. The instruments they needed for a laparoscopy hadn't been sterilized after the last case. They had no choice."

Marla nearly said *this wouldn't have happened if you didn't live in Podunk*, but she clenched her jaw instead. Grace couldn't help it if Port Mariette was where she was born and raised. Marla had only herself to blame.

A machine beeped beside the bed. Grace stared at it for a few moments. "I appreciate that you flew in here for me, but you really didn't have to come all the way from Manhattan."

"You know I'd do anything for you." Marla said it softly, almost apologetically. With so much lost time to make up for, she wanted to help her daughter. Being here was not an imposition.

Grace sighed. "I guess Jesse called you when they were panicking about my B-negative blood."

"Um-hmm." Marla nodded.

"They did manage to get a match somewhere." Grace paused, looking out the window. "A nurse kept asking about my family history. Obviously, I know only yours, not my birth father's." She turned from the window, her eyes now on Marla. "When this is all over, maybe you can tell me more about my birth father. If nothing else, I'd like to learn about his medical history."

"Sure. First, though, we have to get you out of here." Marla had her own opinion about medical care. An early career in nursing had ended abruptly when she gave a patient the wrong med, causing the poor man to leave the facility in a body bag. Marla lost her job and nearly her mind. Ever since then, she never trusted anyone in healthcare. Why should she? They were all just as human as she was.

Grace sighed. "The doctor said I need to stay here at least until tomorrow."

"And after that?"

"I guess I'll have to get some help when Jesse's at work. I'm not supposed to lift more than ten pounds for a couple weeks. Not that I lift a lot of heavy stuff, but I do have to vacuum the spa and restock supplies. Lots of running up and down three flights of stairs."

"How about I stay at the spa for a while? I could fill in for you." Marla owned Victorian Spa and Grace managed it. When Marla was in town she stayed in a spare bedroom, and until marrying Jesse, Grace had lived on the third floor. "I imagine it's really busy right now with people picking up gift cards for Christmas."

"Thanks for the offer, but Hannah and Latoya are more than capable of filling in for me."

Marla wasn't so sure either of them were up to the task. Besides, staff ought to be busy giving facials and massages, not getting bogged down in administrative work.

"I have another idea," Marla said, her voice bright. "How about if you move back to the spa while you're recovering? Jesse would understand. He works such long hours—and didn't you tell me he's in the middle of a huge painting project?"

Grace nodded. "He's putting in ten hours a day doing the parish hall."

"It would take the pressure off him if I took care of you for a while. We could stay in the same rooms, just like before you two got married," Marla said, her voice rising. Now that Grace had gotten married, there would be precious few opportunities to have her daughter all to herself again. Marla couldn't pass up a chance like this. "It would be fun, and remember, I used to be a nurse." She'd never told Grace why she'd left the profession, and certainly wouldn't now.

"Aren't you busy with your foundation?"

Marla shrugged. "Not all that much. Besides, I can work remotely." Last year, she'd made a killing selling Gemstones Gyms, a chain of exclusive fitness centers. A few months afterward, her father died, then her mother—all of which propelled Marla onto the list of America's richest women. "My accountant handles a lot of the foundation's details, and if anything legal comes up, Warren takes care of it."

Grace shrugged. "Thanks for the offer, but I don't think it'll work. If I'm not living in the same house with Jesse, people will think our marriage is already on the rocks. They'll wonder why you're in town again so soon after our wedding too. I don't want to give the Port Mariette rumor mill any material."

Marla tapped her nails on the armrest, in time with the beeping of the machine.

"Appendicitis." A smile sneaked across her face. "Yes, that would be perfect."

Grace cocked her head. "What are you talking about?"

Marla shot up from her chair and aimed her finger at Grace. "You had a ruptured appendix—get it? That's what we'll tell everyone."

Grace perked up. "But don't they fix that with laparoscopic surgery?"

"Ah, don't you remember?—the instruments weren't sterilized." Marla's eyes twinkled. "After a surgery like that, the patient has a long recovery time. You'll need someone to take care of you while Jesse's at work—and that would be *me*!"

'Tis the Time,' 'Tis the Season

Chapter 2

SUZANNE

With a delicate hand, Suzanne Jackson tossed a block of sharp cheddar cheese into her cart at the Port Mariette Dairy Mart, then rounded the corner for eggs. Grocery shopping wasn't how she'd hoped to spend her first day in town, but this summer she and her sister, Andrea, had moved their mother into an assisted living facility. They'd emptied everything edible from her house, so Suzanne would need to do some restocking, even if her stay turned out to be short.

Lucky for Suzanne, she and Andrea hadn't listed the house for sale yet. With her sister overwhelmed with running their art consignment shop, and Suzanne now living in California, who could get around to it? They'd managed to get rid of the accumulated clutter, and while Suzanne was encamped here, maybe she'd have time to clear out the furnishings.

Pondering how to accomplish that, she meandered along the grocery aisle, eventually reaching the eggs, where she picked up a dozen, searched for cracks, and checked the expiration date. Working for an airline most of her career, she'd learned to be fastidious about the smallest detail, and at this little store, perishables weren't likely to move fast.

Farther down the aisle, she spotted a woman who looked exactly like Marla. Tall, elegant, and with those sparkling sapphire earrings—

Oh, that *had* to be Marla. Suzanne plunked the carton of eggs into her cart and scurried down the aisle. "Hey, beautiful!" she called as she neared her friend.

Marla turned. "Suzanne! You're in town too?" They hugged, then Marla glanced around. "Is Rob here with you?"

Suzanne's wavy blonde hair bobbed as she shook her head. "I wish—but he had to stay in California. A contractor's working on some kind of expensive structural issue with our house. Rob said it'd be noisy and dirty, so I may as well go for a visit back home."

She wanted to believe Rob had told her the whole story, but was there more? After all, they'd had one challenge after another since marrying in April, and even at the age of fifty-eight, she still had a hard time trusting any man, especially when it came to money.

Marla tilted her head. "So, what kind of structural issue are you talking about?"

"Rob said it's something to do with the house being located on the side of a cliff. We're in Carmel Highlands, overlooking the ocean. It's pretty steep up there, you know. Maybe we're sliding into the Pacific." Suzanne faked a laugh as she glanced away. "But what do I know about structural engineering?" She shrugged a delicate shoulder. "Anyway, what brought *you* to town?"

"Me? Oh, I came to help Grace at the spa."

"She needs help?" Suzanne scrunched her face.

"Her—her appendix ruptured yesterday."

'Tis the Time,' 'Tis the Season

"Oh, my. Poor thing. How long will it take to recover?"

"A few weeks."

"For a ruptured appendix?" That didn't make sense to Suzanne, but why would Marla lie to her? Perhaps it was that hedge of privacy Marla tended to hide behind—a wall Suzanne sometimes broke through.

"Long story. But not to worry, Grace will be fine."

"Well, I'm glad she's okay." Suzanne continued to examine Marla. "And how about you—how are you doing?" Marla's perfectly made-up face seemed to lack its normal vitality.

"A little weary. I had to drop everything to get here fast."

"And Warren?"

"Busy. He got bored after selling his law practice, so now he's involved in venture capital deals. Big learning curve. He's stressed."

"I imagine your foundation's keeping you busy too."

Marla shrugged. "Talking to people on the phone is the most time-consuming part."

Last year, her foundation paid for renovations to the facades on Port Mariette's Main Street. Marla also came up with ideas to draw visitors too. Almost singlehandedly, she turned the town around.

"Well, as long as we're both in town for a while," Suzanne said, "why don't we make the most of it?" Since moving to the West Coast earlier this year, she'd missed her old high school friends more than expected. Rachel had been her constant friend since kindergarten, and although Marla had lived in Port Mariette only their senior year, the three of them became inseparable—until they parted right after graduation.

Last year's reunion brought them together again for the first time in forty years, when Suzanne had just lost her job, Marla was searching for her daughter, and Rachel had unexpectedly become a widow. Their trials bonded them anew, and even though they now lived miles apart, they managed to keep in touch with visits and occasional calls.

"The three of us need to get together right away," Suzanne said, excitement in her voice.

Marla pulled out a credit card as they neared the checkout lane. "I agree. Who knows how long we'll be together this time?"

"How about we pop over to Food 'n Fuel right now? Rachel will be shocked to see both of us showing up unexpectedly." Suzanne grinned a little giddily. Surprises were one of her favorite things.

After checking out, they loaded the groceries into their cars and wended their way along the icy sidewalk to Food 'n Fuel.

Inside, Rachel's oldest son Pete greeted them from behind the counter.

"Nice to see you again, ladies. Sorry, but you just missed my mom. She's attending a board meeting. Port Mariette Business Association." He sounded proud of his mother, and for good reason.

Earlier this year, when the town needed to band together to protect its business interests, Suzanne and Marla had persuaded Rachel to become PMBA's secretary. Even though all three of them owned businesses there, only Rachel lived in town.

"She's been keeping both of us in the loop about local business activities," Marla said.

Pete grinned. "Did you know she's PMBA's president now?"

"You're kidding." Suzanne's eyes widened. Rachel hadn't been involved in her family's business until Stan's death last April forced her into action. "What happened to Mary Frances?"

"She's retiring. Moving to Florida."

"Mary Frances retiring?" Marla's face registered surprise.

Suzanne gasped. "I never thought I'd see the day." Other than Marla, Mary Frances was the most ambitious woman Suzanne knew. If she wasn't working on a real estate deal, she was networking to land the next one.

"Yeah, it came as a surprise." Pete put his elbows on the counter. "She told my mom real estate isn't the best line of work for someone with joint problems—at least not in Port Mariette where all the homes are two-stories with basements."

"Will her office be vacant?" Suzanne knew she might sound like a vulture, but she'd been looking to expand Creations on Main, the art shop she and her sister jointly owned, and Mary Frances's office was right across the street. They could move all the paintings and sculptures there and keep the craft-type items and art classes at the current location.

"It's already taken," Pete said. "My girlfriend Lindsey is opening her second location there. She's been wanting to expand her real estate business into Port Mariette ever since we got the new highway exit. As you can imagine, Lyondale doesn't generate a lot of sales."

"Wow. That happened fast," Suzanne said flatly. So much for keeping them in the loop.

Pete nodded. "My mom and Mary Frances have gotten a little tight, being PMBA officers and all. As soon as she told Mom about her retirement plans, Mom told Lindsey, "You gotta jump on an opportunity like that."

"Indeed." Suzanne's tone was chilly, but Pete didn't seem to notice. She grabbed a couple to-go meals from a nearby refrigerated case and plopped them on the counter. "Well, I hope she never runs out of time to cook. Anything she makes beats cooking myself."

Pete talked as he tapped on the terminal. "That'll be seventeen dollars."

Suzanne picked up one of the bags and put it back in the display case. "On second thought, I think one of these will suffice." With her income from the art shop erratic and no idea how much that project with the house would end up costing, she should avoid frivolous spending.

"Sure, that'll be eight-fifty," Pete said, tapping into the terminal again.

"Rachel's probably reeling from her new responsibilities at PMBA," Marla said. "That's a lot more than she signed up for."

"But I'm sure she'll adjust." Suzanne reached over the counter and grabbed her purchase. She glanced at Pete before heading to the door. "Would you let her know we stopped by?"

"We can't wait to get together with her," Marla said, following behind Suzanne.

"You bet." Pete saluted them goodbye.

On the way back to their cars, Suzanne said, "Rachel must be really busy. I can't believe she accepted the presidency without calling us to talk about it first."

"That's so unlike her," Marla said. "Maybe it's Mary Frances's influence on her."

"Could be. After all, Rachel wouldn't have been involved in PMBA at all if you and I hadn't come up with the concept, the name, and the bylaws—"

"Warren did the bylaws," Marla said, interrupting Suzanne's rant.

"Of course, but that was because he's in a relationship with you. And then, you and I practically forced her to become secretary."

Just ahead of them, a hunter green pickup pulled into a parking spot and beeped.

"That's Mitch," Marla said, accelerating her pace.

As they neared his truck, Mitch Mitchell rolled down the window, pulled off his ballcap, and poked his head out. "Well, hello, ladies. What a nice surprise to see you two back in town."

Both of them had gotten to know Mitch well the past year or so. This past summer, he led the effort to remove the fallen pine trees threatening to undo the town's Fourth of July arts festival, an event chaired by Suzanne. Before that, his contracting firm had handled multiple projects for Marla and her foundation.

She always said the man could do anything, and Suzanne had to agree.

"Nice to see you again," Suzanne said.

"Hi, Mitch." Marla smiled at him broadly then turned to Suzanne. "You know, there are plenty of houses here in Port Mariette on the hills overlooking the river. Why don't you see what Mitch knows about structural problems on a cliffside house?"

Suzanne opened her mouth to speak, just as her phone pinged with a text. She glanced at the screen.

"It's Rob," she said, raising her hand to her heart.

Call me. When you're alone.

Chapter 3

RACHEL

Rachel Baran, the newly appointed president of Port Mariette Business Association, sat up straight as her ironing board at the head of the conference room table in the executive suite of Starlight Country Club. Normally, she would have worn one of her pink polo shirts with the Food 'n Fuel logo, but today she needed to command respect, so instead, she wore a brand-new black one.

She should have washed it before wearing it today, though. The scratchy fabric was making her itch all over. Or maybe it was the black dye—was it bleeding onto her armpits?

Nine irritated men sat around the table, most of them older than her and every one of them more experienced in business than she was. She took a few deep breaths, scratched an itch on her side, and said a silent Hail Mary. She'd do anything to contain her nerves in front of PMBA's officers and board members.

Goodness knows, these men didn't think she was up to the task. Without Mary Frances backing her, she never would have made it to the top of the organization. Like a bunch of stubborn politicians, they'd all dug in their heels and refused to give her a majority vote—until Mary Frances pointed out that according to the bylaws, if a current president resigns, he or she has authority to appoint a replacement for the duration of the term—and to the men's amazement, she chose Rachel.

Now, she had six months to prove herself. She was determined to do just that.

Surely she was up for it. In high school, she'd been captain of the majorettes and vice president of the home ec club. She'd raised a family and kept her marriage together, and after Stan died, she overhauled his service station, turning it into a popular art deco style gas station where customers stopped by to take selfies along with buying gas and food. Pete ran the counter, and Rachel prepared their moneymaker—the meals to go. Every single day, she had decisions to make, people to please, changes to make. Maybe no one had noticed how she'd grown, but in the coming months, she'd show them.

She rapped the gavel twice, savoring the formality and reveling in the power the presidency afforded her. "I call this meeting of PMBA to order." She waited patiently, knowing men liked to yammer just as much as women.

In time, the room quieted.

"Our first order of business is the election of a new secretary to replace me." She had to hold back a smug smile.

"Aw, Rachel, can't you just take the notes?" Herbie Herbinger said, twirling his pen. A busy man, he owned a lot of the properties on Main Street and had no tolerance for wasting time.

"Besides, that's a woman's job," said Joe the barber, pursing his thin lips until they disappeared.

'Tis the Time,' 'Tis the Season

It didn't surprise her that Joe would object to doing what he considered women's work. At his barber shop, he cut only men's hair. If a woman wanted so much as a trim of her bangs, he sent her down the street to Sharon's place, Hair & Care.

Nor did it surprise Rachel that every man in the room sounded their agreement with Joe. This was Port Mariette, after all, not Manhattan. Even Marla, the smartest businesswoman Rachel knew, wouldn't know how to deal with a situation like this.

"Sorry to disappoint you, gentlemen," Rachel said, "but on page six, second paragraph, our bylaws state that officers can hold only one position." Thank goodness Mary Frances had taught her to do her homework in anticipation of the men's pushback. "Since I have been duly appointed president"—she paused to look each one of them dead in the eye—"That means someone else has to be secretary." She shrugged. "It is what it is, fellas. So, who's it gonna be?"

She sat still, waiting for their childish groaning to die down. After a long minute, Herbie spoke up. "I'll do it." He clicked his pen and jotted a note on his tablet.

"Thank you, Herbie. Let the record show that Herbie Herbinger has volunteered to be secretary." She looked around the room, her chin held high. "All in favor, say *Aye*."

Herbie heaved a sigh as he recorded the unanimous response.

"Let's move on to the next item on our agenda." Rachel flipped to the next page. "Something a bit more fun than electing a new secretary—the Christmas Eve parade. As you know, we still need a Santa Claus."

Walt Celinski, publisher of the *Port Mariette Gazette*, stood up. "I hereby nominate Herbie Herbinger to be

Santa Claus." He said it with a straight face, but a ripple of laughter rolled through the room. She was tempted to giggle right along with them, but Mary Frances had warned her she needed to break that high school habit if she wanted to be taken seriously. Easy for Mary Frances to say. She rarely cracked a smile.

Herbie's lunar face turned a little red, but his eyes twinkled, and he patted his ample belly.

"First, secretary, now Santa Claus. Does it get any better?" He shook his head, faking defeat. "I accept the nomination."

"Thank you, Herbie," Rachel said, amid the banter. "All right, any new business?"

Dr. Hess, the town's elderly dentist, leaned forward in his seat. "Just like each one of you, I've lived in Port Mariette my whole life. We all remember how our population sharply declined when the steel and coal industries left town. Then last year when that new highway exit was constructed and Main Street was renovated, the population increased."

Rachel nodded a little vigorously, hoping to speed him along.

"Lately, though, our growth has been leveling off," Dr. Hess said, "and let's remember, Port Mariette has a high percentage of senior citizens. You know what that means. Lipton's Funeral Home is busier than ever."

Barry Lipton acknowledged the statement with a nod.

Dr. Hess smacked a fist on the table for emphasis. "We need to get young people to settle down here, raise their families, and keep our population strong. I think PMBA ought to focus on attracting young people. I need more people with cavities—not seniors with a mouthful of false teeth."

Joe piped up. "And I need men who have hair."

'Tis the Time, 'Tis the Season

While all the men laughed, Rachel glanced at the clock. The meeting was lasting longer than she expected. Poor Pete, alone at Food 'n Fuel. She needed to get back there.

"Thank you for raising that topic, Dr. Hess. I'll put it on the agenda for our next board meeting. For now, we've got to focus on the Christmas parade."

Dr. Hess opened his mouth to protest, but Herbie intervened. "Anyone want to be Mrs. Claus?"

The men guffawed. A few of them looked at Rachel expectantly.

Curvy as she was, Rachel knew she'd make a perfect Mrs. Claus, but she wasn't about to volunteer for one more thing. Maybe Mary Frances would agree to do it, if she'd still be in town. After all, she and Herbie had been dating for a while.

With no suggestions offered, Herbie finally said, "All right, then, why don't we adjourn."

Rachel rapped the gavel. The room emptied in a snap. Every one of them had a business to run.

On the way to her car, she pulled out her phone and pressed the number for Tony Mastriano. Both of them now widowed, they met again at last year's high school reunion and got around to dating this summer. Now that he'd opened his Sweet Treats shop on Main Street, they were on their way to becoming Port Mariette's power couple.

"How'd the meeting go?" Tony asked.

"Smooth as melted chocolate." Rachel giggled, then she told him how Herbie had stepped up to take on both the secretary and Santa roles.

"Doesn't surprise me," Tony said. "The 80/20 rule."

"What's that?"

"Eighty percent of the work is done by twenty percent of the people."

Rachel had never heard of that rule before, but it made sense. Between Tony and PMBA, she was sure learning a lot—and loving it. What a thrill to be coming into her own at this stage of life. She'd teach everyone to not underestimate her.

After finishing her conversation with Tony, she called her son. "I'm on my way." She hoped he'd found time for a bathroom break.

"No need to rush. I'm fine." Pete said. "Hey, your high school girlfriends stopped by. Suzanne and Marla."

"They're *both* in town? I didn't know either one of them would be visiting." Rachel bit her lower lip. She'd been too busy to let them know about the changes at PMBA. On the other hand, they'd been too busy to let her know they'd be in town.

"Yeah, they're both here. They said they want to get together with you."

"Oh, boy." Rachel rubbed her forehead. "I wonder how I'll squeeze them in."

Chapter 4

MARLA

As soon as Suzanne left, Mitch hopped out of his truck and landed in front of Marla. Tall as she was, Mitch still had several inches on her.

"In town again so soon?" he said, a sandy eyebrow raised. "You were here just a couple months ago when Grace and Jesse *succumbed to love.*" He chuckled as he said the last few words.

"You really get a kick out of using big words, don't you?" Marla smirked. "Trying to impress someone?"

"You, Marla. Only you. The swan in the coal mine."

That's what Mitch had called her when they'd first bumped into one another at the Dairy Mart last year, her first visit to Port Mariette since high school. The man did have a way with words, odd as they might be, and at least he had the guts to say them out loud. Warren, on the other hand, was verbose in a court room, but when it came to Marla, an occasional little love note was his limit—and the one he'd slipped in her carryon before she left yesterday did not contain the usual sweet talk. She was still not sure what Warren was driving at.

"To answer your question," Marla said, forcing her voice to sound convincing, "Grace needs me for a while."

"That's pretty vague." He cocked his head and waited for details.

"It's not a big deal." Marla gave him a quick summary of Grace's emergency surgery, hoping she'd fooled him with her explanation. If she could convince Mitch, she could probably get away with the coverup anywhere in town.

Mitch rubbed his stubbled chin but said nothing.

She continued her story. "She'll be out of commission for a while, so I offered to fill in for her at the spa until she's feeling better."

He put a hand on his hip, as if he knew something wasn't adding up. "If you're supposed to be running the spa, how come you're waltzing around on Main Street?"

"Good question." Marla said with a hint of sarcasm. "Our first client today isn't due until four o'clock."

"Four o'clock? Hardly worth the cost of heating all those high-ceilinged rooms.

"I know. Bookings are really thin right now."

"But I guess that's to be expected this time of year," he said. "People are probably too busy Christmas shopping. No time for primping."

"You think so?" She'd expected a more probing response from him. Over the past year and a half, she and Mitch had teamed up to transform her aunt's Victorian mansion into a spa and then they renovated Main Street. They'd golfed and dined together, and once, she even visited his church. All the while, they'd had many conversations—business, personal, even arguments—all of which had led to an unlikely friendship with a man who understood her better than anyone else she'd ever known. Letting down her guard didn't come naturally to Marla, but with Mitch, she had come to feel safe, free to be herself.

"What's Grace's explanation for the drop-off in business?" Mitch asked.

"I haven't asked. I can't bother her with questions while she's still in the hospital."

"Understandable."

"You haven't heard anything bad about the spa, have you?" Marla held her breath, wondering what he might tell her.

"Boy, you're sure asking the right person. I get my nails done there every week."

Marla chortled, then turned serious again. "How about Grace? Have you heard anything going on with her? There might be something she's afraid to tell me."

"Grace?" He shook his head. "You'd have to talk to someone in the know. Like Penny. By the way, have you heard she's mayor again?"

"Seriously? After all she did?" Marla could hardly believe it. Penny had tried to use her position as mayor to finagle her way out of bankruptcy, and when she got caught, she took revenge on the town by posting anonymous reviews on the local businesses. Lucky for her, the town decided her mental state required therapy, not prosecution.

"Yep." Mitch nodded. "Word is she followed through with her counseling, so when no one else wanted to be mayor, she raised her hand and got herself reappointed."

Marla shook her head. "Such a strange little town, Port Mariette."

"People are strange everywhere." Mitch inclined his lean body against the spotless truck. "Or haven't you noticed?"

Warren's unsettling note came to her mind. "Oh, believe me, I've noticed."

Her phone rang. "It's Grace." Marla took the call. "Everything okay?"

"They want to discharge me today," Grace said, anxiety rippling in her voice. "Jesse's in the middle of his painting project. Can you come get me?"

"Sure." A knowing smile spread across her face. "Where do you want me to take you?"

Chapter 5

SUZANNE

Suzanne backed onto Main Street and sped along the few blocks to her mother's house, all the while wondering why Rob asked her to be alone when she called him. She'd only been gone a day—what could have happened?

Is he sick? Injured? In the hospital? Did his daughter get fired from that awful high-pressure job? Or maybe his son is having new mental health challenges. That would be unfortunate but not too much of a surprise, considering how Kevin's issues had upended their honeymoon earlier this year.

She jumped out of the car, forgetting all about the groceries in the trunk, and dashed across the snow-covered lawn to reach the front door. She pressed Rob's number on her phone as she slammed the door behind her.

"Thanks for calling so fast," Rob said, sounding weary.

"What is it? What's wrong?" She sank into a chair, waiting for the blow.

"It's ... it's about that contractor I hired."

"Did he fall down the cliff?" She didn't have any idea what Rob was driving at.

"He's fine. It's the house." Rob paused. "The structural issues are worse than expected."

"How much worse?" She'd tried to sound in control of her emotions but knew she was failing.

"It's a little complicated."

"Or do you mean *expensive*?" Her voice rose.

"Both. Complicated *and* expensive."

Rob droned on for several minutes, explaining minutiae about concrete-and-steel pilings. It all flew right over Suzanne's head. Why couldn't he get right to the point at a time like this?

"Can't you just tell me in plain English—what did the contractor tell you?" She spaced out the words as she said them, articulating every syllable.

Rob remained silent for a moment, as if condensing his thoughts before responding. "When a house is built on a cliffside, there's always a risk of the land becoming unstable." He heaved a sigh. "Unfortunately, some fissures have developed in the house's foundation."

"Can't the contractor glue it back together? Like, with some special cement? Or maybe you could look on one of those AI sites and try to find a less expensive solution."

"I wish I could," Rob said. "It's not that simple. The problem underneath has to be addressed. Neither glue nor AI will do it. Look, Suzanne, this contractor has a stellar reputation here in Carmel Highlands. He knows what needs to be done, and he made it clear the work is significant."

"So," Suzanne said, "that means it will be expensive." She went silent for a moment, then brightened. "But your homeowner's insurance will cover it, right?"

A long, loud breath came from Rob's end.

Suzanne sat straight up. "You do have homeowner's insurance, don't you?"

Chapter 6

RACHEL

Still basking in the glow of her first meeting as PMBA president, Rachel scampered through the back door of Food 'n Fuel, giggling and dancing around like she was still a majorette.

At the counter, Pete stood watching, laughing. "I guess PMBA went well?"

"Better than expected." She concluded her dance. "So, anything going on around here?"

"Just the usual. It's been steady. And we're almost out of your sausage lasagna."

"No problem. I was planning to make a few pans today."

Pete moved from behind the counter, his face now serious. "Got a minute to talk?"

Was Pete going to wreck her happy mood? She glanced around. Outside, two cars were filling up, but there were no customers inside the store.

"What's up?" she said, steeling herself.

"Lindsey and I are having dinner in Pittsburgh tonight. At Tony's restaurant."

"You mean Tony's *son's* restaurant, right?" Rachel corrected him with a raised finger. Tony's son had taken over Signore's, enabling Tony to move to Port Mariette and open a candy shop. He claimed it had always been his dream, but Rachel suspected Tony could no longer keep up with the demands of a big place like Signore's. No matter. Tony had moved to Port Mariette, he made candy like nobody's business, and he always had time for her.

"Yeah," Pete said, "That's what I mean, Tony's son's restaurant."

"Why drive so far for an Italian dinner? Why not Dom's?" Her loyalty rested with any restaurant that bought her prepared meals—even though they all passed it off as their own. At Signore's, Tony used to buy tons of her Italian meals and pierogies too, but now his son wanted everything made on site. Tony assured her that would change in time, but until then, Signore's would not be getting any recommendations from her, no siree. Dom, on the other hand, still bought plenty of her Italian dishes.

"Why not Dom's? Well, uh ..." Suddenly Pete's face had an impish look.

Rachel's mouth dropped open. "You're gonna pop the question, aren't you?"

He broke into a wide grin. "Yep." Pete reached into his pants pocket and pulled out a black velvet ring box. "Wanna see it?"

"Open it!" Rachel put her hand on her heart as he flipped the lid. Of all her sons, Pete most resembled Stan, and for a moment, she slipped back in time, remembering when he had charmingly bumbled his way through his marriage proposal. She'd accepted on the spot, but even so, she'd always wished Stan had added a little romance to the moment. Pete would do better, she hoped.

"Do you think Lindsey will like it?" Gingerly, he handed the ring to Rachel.

'Tis the Time,' Tis the Season

Rachel twisted it in the light, causing all three small diamonds to glitter. "It's gorgeous. Trust me, she'll love it." She handed back the ring.

"There's something else I wanted to talk about with you." Pete shuffled his feet as he put the ring box back into his pocket. "You know how much I've always wanted to have kids."

"Uh-huh." She nodded. Pete's first wife wanted a career, not children. It broke his heart and ruined their marriage.

"Lindsey feels the same way."

"Wonderful."

"We plan to start a family as soon as we get married."

Rachel clapped her hands together in excitement. "Grandkids right here in Port Mariette—I can't wait!"

"Right—but it's expensive to raise children."

Rachel gasped. Was Pete about to tell her he'd be leaving Food 'n Fuel for a regular job? That he'd be moving away? How far? Farther away than her other sons?

He leaned closer and dropped his voice, even though no one else was around. "You know how you told me Esther is going to be closing her antique shop?"

Rachel nodded, wondering why Pete had changed the subject. Poor Esther. Pancreatic cancer. Only months to go. Esther didn't want anyone to know, but she'd confided in Rachel. After all, Esther said, the president of PMBA ought to be aware of a transition like that on Main Street, and besides, they'd developed a bond over many years of owning side-by-side businesses.

"Of course. But what's Esther got to do with raising kids?"

"She stopped over here this morning while you were at PMBA."

"How's she doing?" Although mildly annoyed by Pete's run-around, Rachel was still curious about Esther.

"Seemed a little weak," Pete said.

"Has she found someone to buy her business?"

"Yeah."

"Who? Inez?" Always complaining her handmade dolls didn't get enough shelf space at Creations on Main, Inez was the logical person.

A smile curled Pete's lips.

"C'mon, who is it?" Rachel clasped her hands, eager to hear who would be moving in next door to Food 'n Fuel.

Pete poked his chest. "Me."

"You?" She cocked her head as her mind processed the implications of Pete leaving her business. She forced a smile. "Well, I guess I shouldn't be surprised. Look at all your accomplishments here at Food 'n Fuel. You've probably already dreamed up something spectacular."

Pete preened. "Well, I hope so. The way I look at it, Esther's inventory of antiques isn't worth a lot. Mainly she's got old furniture from senior citizens who can't stay in their houses because of all the steps. I could buy her out for a reasonable price, then over time, I'd add things people are really interested in."

"Like what?"

"Road signs, old toys, trading cards. You know, all those odd things people collect then store in their basements. Vintage stuff."

"Too bad Suzanne already got rid of all her mom's junk."

"Yeah, that would have been perfect. But there are plenty of other crammed basements and attics in this town. Over in Dunham City and Lyondale too. Lindsey tells me some of the amazing stuff she sees when she gets a new listing. She has to tell people to get rid of all the clutter before they put their house on the market, but they don't

'Tis the Time,' Tis the Season

know how to do it. They need an easy way to unload it and make a little money on it too. That's where I come in."

"Boy, your mind has been churning all morning, hasn't it?" Rachel giggled.

He nodded with excitement. "I already have a name for the place—*Treasures from the Attic*." Pete walked over to the wall behind him and put a hand on it. "We could put a door with a window right here so I can go back and forth between businesses."

"We'd still probably have to hire another employee, but I do love your idea." Adding staff would hurt her bottom line, but at least Pete wasn't leaving her high and dry.

"Best of all, it would basically double my income, and that's the goal."

"You have such a good mind for business." Rachel tapped the side of her head a few times. "Just like Marla."

"Thanks, Mom. That reminds me. Now that your friends are in town, do you think you'll be getting together with them soon? I was hoping you could run my concept by Marla before I move forward, or grease the wheels before I call her." Pete looked at her imploringly. "Can you do it?"

Rachel would never disappoint her son. "I'll squeeze that in tonight." How she'd manage to do it, she didn't know. It had been weeks since she'd even said a rosary, much less cleared a whole evening to have dinner with two old girlfriends.

Chapter 7

MARLA

Marla was eager to get Grace out of Hope Hospital, yet she took her time finishing her conversation with Mitch before driving over there. Just because a nurse said they'd be discharging Grace today didn't mean it would happen anytime soon. Besides, it had been a while since she'd seen Mitch.

Eventually, Marla pulled her coupe into the crowded hospital parking lot and found a spot far from the entrance. She'd worn a pair of leather boots, but Gucci was not a brand designed for trekking in rock salt.

Entering the building, she stomped a few times on the black floor mat, although the damage had been done. If she'd be in town for a while, she'd have to buy some practical footwear.

She strode into Room 311 and found Grace sitting in the bedside chair, still in her hospital gown, hands folded in her lap. *Was Grace praying?* If she was, Marla didn't want to interrupt her, nor did she want an invitation to join together in prayer. Not that Marla lacked faith. She just didn't have as much as others seemed to, and she'd always been too busy to figure out why.

Her eyes sad, Grace looked up at Marla standing in the doorway. "Thanks for coming. A nurse just told me it would be a while longer. I should have called to let you know."

"That's okay. I figured it'd be a while, and I don't mind waiting." Marla hunched closer. "How are you feeling today?"

"Eh." Grace shrugged. "Physically, I'm still in some pain. But the emotional pain—that's what's worse."

"I can only imagine." She knew better than to ask any questions. An inquisition would only serve to silence Grace. Marla waited for her to continue.

"Funny how life can change so quickly," Grace mused, her eyes now having a far-away look. "All those years I hadn't seen Jesse—since high school—then he shows up here in Port Mariette, and boom—I fall in love, get married, get pregnant." She rested a hand on her midsection. "And now this."

Where was this conversation headed? Unsure, Marla replied in a neutral voice. "You've experienced quite a turn of events." She sounded like a businesswoman, not a doting mother, and she knew it.

Grace seemed not to notice. "At my age," she continued, "I never thought a story like this could happen."

Marla perched herself on the side of the bed. "Jesse's a good man," she said, hoping to steer the conversation toward cheerful topics like a good mother should. "I can see that you two are happy together."

"We are." Grace smoothed her wrinkled hospital gown. "One of the attractions we had right off the bat is having the same priorities for our lives. We've both always wanted to have a big family, so even at our age, we decided to try to have a baby. We thought we might even be able to have two before it was too late."

"I see." A weak response, but Marla didn't know what else to say.

"After this, we'll never have even one baby. It's just so ..." Grace's voice trailed off.

"It's so sad. I wish I could make it better for you." With all the money Marla had, this was a tragedy she could never fix.

A tear trailed down Grace's cheek. "Sorry. I'm so emotional right now. Being here in the hospital where I was born—and now losing my chance at having a baby of my own—it's just a bit much." She wiped away the tear. "I think all those questions about my family history stirred up my emotions too." She sniffed. "It's hard, but I think it's good to talk about what I'm feeling—even if it is through tears."

Marla got up to close the door then returned to the edge of the bed. "You know, being here in this hospital has stirred up my memories too. Your adoption has always been such an emotional topic for me."

"Believe me, I get it." Grace nodded. "You met my parents. You know they were wonderful. But I have to admit, once I learned I had been adopted, I never felt quite the same. I always wondered, wasn't I good enough for my birth parents? Why did they abandon me? I always had so many questions about my past. I was glad when you came searching for me last year."

Marla leaned over and touched Grace's hand. "Would you like to know about the circumstances of your adoption? The whole truth, not just what I told you last year when we finally met?"

Grace nodded, her big brown eyes growing wide. "Yes, I would."

Marla paused a moment before beginning. Deep discussions with her daughter were rare. She needed to choose her words carefully.

"I'm sure you remember, I was only sixteen." Marla shifted on the bed. "Unsure of myself. Not very popular. I was taller than a lot of the boys. I felt gawky." She looked at Grace, still a knock-out at forty-two, and wondered if she'd gone through that same awkward stage.

"One night," Marla said, "there was a dance in the gym after a football game. We'd won, and everyone was celebrating. Some kids had snuck alcohol into the gym. All around me, kids were drinking. Somehow, I managed to get drunk too. After the dance, a big group of kids stumbled over to the golf course to continue drinking, and being drunk myself, I didn't hesitate to tag along."

Marla brushed some imaginary lint from her slacks. She needed a moment to gather the courage to continue.

"Before long, kids all around me were making out. I felt like such a loser. But then a guy I hardly knew pushed me down on the ground and started kissing me. I just went along with it. Then at some point, I managed to get myself home."

Marla got up and looked out the window. "I'm embarrassed to tell you this, but you need to know—I was never sure if he was your birth father, or if it was someone else. I just don't remember." Marla hung her head, too ashamed to look her daughter in the eye. "I had a blackout, you see. I never figured out if it was because of drinking too much or if my mind was blocking a terrible memory."

"Oh my gosh." Grace covered her mouth with her fingertips.

Marla felt herself tensing all over. Had she said too much?

"How horrible that must have been." Grace slowly shook her head.

"I wish I had a better story for you, Grace—young love, that sort of thing—but I didn't want to lie. You need to know the truth, or at least as much as I remember."

"I ... I'd always hoped I came about as a result of puppy love," Grace said. "Probably every adopted kid feels that way. To be honest, it makes me a little sad and even angry at my birth father, whoever he is—but I do understand why you couldn't keep me." She paused. "I guess I'll never know anything about my birth father's medical history. If I go digging on one of those ancestry sites, I'm not sure I'd want to find him. Or maybe he wouldn't want to be found."

"It's up to you, of course. You have reasons why you want to find him as well as reasons why you don't." At least while she was alive, Marla hoped Grace would never connect with her birth father. That was a memory she'd rather not resurrect.

Grace stared out the window. "Thank you for telling me the whole story. That must have been hard to do."

Marla nodded, thankful Grace had reacted so well.

They sat in silence for a few moments, then Grace said, "As long as we're having this kind of conversation, maybe I should tell you something about me."

Marla's eyes widened with concern. "No matter what it is, I still love you."

"I know that." Grace stared at her lap. "Back in high school, I had a terrible experience. It's colored my whole life." She looked up at the ceiling and sighed. "I guess I'll just say it—my senior year, I ... I got pregnant."

Marla couldn't help it. She gasped.

Grace took a long breath and continued. "I should have known better. I was dating a guy I really liked, but when I told him I missed a period, he freaked out. Me? I panicked. I couldn't tell my parents. You know they were such devoted Catholics. It would have crushed them." She covered her face with a hand. "So I ... I ... oh, I'm so ashamed to tell you." Grace looked up, her eyes filled with grief. "I had an abortion." She sobbed. "I killed my baby."

Marla's body froze, but her mind raced. *A grandchild. I would have been a grandmother.*

Chapter 8

SUZANNE

That evening, sitting across from Marla at Dom's Restaurant, Suzanne tapped her nails on the white tablecloth. All her career, she'd gotten weekly manicures, but now that she'd become an artist, she cared more about her paintings than having her nails done. Besides, the solvents and cleaners she used quickly ruined even the best manicure. Small price to pay for such a fulfilling line of work.

Once again, Suzanne checked the time. "It's not like Rachel to be late," she said to Marla. "I wonder if something's happened to her. Maybe I should call her."

As far as Suzanne was concerned, Rachel couldn't arrive soon enough. Although Suzanne was irritated her long-time friend hadn't kept her in the loop about Mary Frances's vacant office space, she'd still welcome having Rachel at the table. For whatever reason, Marla was not herself tonight. Her mood had changed from this morning, and she was not willing to discuss whatever was dragging her down.

These past twenty minutes, for lack of another topic, Suzanne had filled the time with details about Rob's failure to have proper coverage for something called *ground movement*. Before today, she hadn't even known it was possible for someone to self-insure their house, much less what possessed Rob to take such a chance. The engineering problem involved technical jargon she couldn't grasp and worst of all, fixing it would cost a small fortune. All this made for a pretty boring conversation, but at least it gave her a chance to vent.

"Still waiting for a third?" The pony-tailed server asked again.

With relief, Suzanne pointed to the entrance. "That's her coming in the door right now." Rachel, the only one of the three who'd lived her entire life in Port Mariette, had a way of grounding them. Just what Suzanne needed right now ... and maybe Marla too. Plus, Rachel loved girl talk. Things were looking up.

"Hi, sorry I'm late," Rachel said, dusting some snow from her parka and fluffing her streaky blonde hair, but not offering an excuse for her tardiness. She hung the jacket over the back of her chair and said to the server, "I'll have a merlot."

"A merlot?" Suzanne couldn't help but question the choice. "I've never seen you drink anything but beer. Ever."

Rachel shrugged. "Tony's influence. He's big into reds."

"Ready for another?" The server arched an eyebrow at Suzanne and Marla.

"We're good for now." Suzanne was thankful Marla didn't ask for a second glass of wine or something even stronger. Marla might look like the picture of health, but Suzanne knew all about Marla's mini-stroke last year and didn't want her having a repeat incident.

"I'll be right back for your orders," the server said, making it sound more like a command than attentive customer service.

'Tis the Time, 'Tis the Season

"It's great to see you both," Rachel gushed, "but I'm surprised you're back in town so soon. Anything going on I should know about?" She flicked her cloth napkin and spread it across her lap.

Marla updated them on Grace's condition, giving few details. She still seemed to be in a funk.

Then Suzanne explained what brought her to town. When Rachel stifled a yawn, Suzanne got the message. "Insurance for ground movement isn't exactly an exciting topic. How about you tell us what's new with you, Rachel?"

The server appeared with the merlot, interrupting their conversation. "Are we ready to order?" She clicked her pen.

They placed their orders, and after the server departed, Rachel sniffed her wine. She took a dramatic sip. "Oh, that's so smooth. It will pair well with the beef ravioli." She patted her lips delicately with her napkin.

Suzanne gawked at her. *Who was this new Rachel?*

"What's happening with me, you asked?" Rachel put her napkin back on her lap and pressed it smooth. "Just about everything. Let's see ..." First she told them about the plans for Port Mariette's first annual Christmas parade. "We'll have it the afternoon of Christmas Eve so people can buy plenty of last-minute gifts. Herbie will be Santa." She looked at Marla. "Would you be willing to sing some Christmas carols?"

"If I'm in town," Marla said. "Right now, I'm not sure how long I'll be here."

"If you can't do it, I guess I could ask the choir from church." Rachel tapped a finger on her chin, then she turned to Suzanne.

"You did such a phenomenal job with the arts festival back in July. I was wondering if you could help with the vendors for the Christmas parade. Some of them need to up their game with their holiday decorations."

Suzanne had whipped together the Fourth of July event in only eleven days and vowed she'd never again be in such a position. Now, Rachel was asking her to help with another event? No way.

"I don't have any idea how long I'll be here," Suzanne said. "I can't commit to anything like that." Her voice didn't sound the least bit sorry, and she didn't care.

"Maybe your sister Andrea can do it. I'll give her a call."

"You can give it a try, but I doubt she'll be able to do it." Suzanne took a sip of her wine. She could hardly get Andrea to balance their checkbook.

"And Pete said he told you about Mary Frances retiring," Rachel said. "I can't believe I'm president now."

"You've come a long way, baby," Suzanne said, playfully poking Rachel in the arm.

"Good for you." Marla said with little enthusiasm, her mind seemingly on something else.

Rachel then launched into a monologue about how *wonderful* things were with her and Tony, the places they'd visited, the special moments they'd shared.

Hearing the romantic details made Suzanne squirm. Tony had never been like that when they dated in high school. Or maybe her memories of him had faded—although she vividly remembered him dumping her right before the senior prom. Who could forget that? And now he was dating Rachel. Life didn't get much weirder than that.

Rachel raved about Tony a while longer then launched into the latest news about PMBA. "Warren sure thought of everything when he wrote those bylaws for us."

Marla smirked. "Don't be so impressed. He used boilerplate."

"Well, even if it was boilerplate, it was the right wording for me. Tell him I appreciate it."

Marla gave a brief nod.

'Tis the Time,' Tis the Season

Their food arrived, and Suzanne said a blessing, shorter than usual. Praying didn't suit her mood right now. She missed Rob, Marla was acting strangely, and Rachel had morphed into someone Suzanne barely recognized.

"I have some really good news," said Rachel, with a dramatic wave of her hand. "But you have to keep it secret for at least a day." Without waiting for their assent, she leaned toward them, her eyes wide. "Pete's going to propose to Lindsey!"

"How wonderful." Suzanne forced a little joy into her voice. *You'd think she was announcing her own engagement to Tony.* Would that be the next item on this evening's agenda?

"And that's not all, ladies." Rachel took another sip of wine before leaning forward again. "This is confidential too." She explained about Esther's deteriorating health. "Pete's going to buy her out and change the name to *Treasures from the Attic*."

Suzanne shoved a big bite of chicken parm into her mouth so she wouldn't be tempted to say anything. Everyone in town should have had the chance to make an offer on that shop. She'd missed out on getting Mary Frances's real estate office across the street, and now the antique shop just a few doors away from Creations on Main would be Pete's.

Rachel lifted her fork and pointed it toward Marla. "I'm sure Pete will be reaching out to you while you're in town. I told him it'd be a good idea to pick your brain about his new business."

Marla seemed to nod, but Suzanne wasn't quite sure. She looked her over. Her lips looked a little strange and her posture seemed stiff.

Suzanne gasped. *Oh, no—a mini-stroke! That's it—Marla must be having another one.*

Chapter 9

RACHEL

A light coating of fresh wet snow lay on the roads when Rachel left Dom's. Having had more wine than she probably should have, and still shaken over the possibility of Marla having another mini-stroke, Rachel knew enough to drive out of the parking lot with extra caution. She'd intended to go straight home after dining with her friends, but once in her car, she decided to call Tony instead. Without waiting for him to say hello, she whimpered, "I need a hug."

"Come on over, sweetie." Tony replied instantly. "I'll be waiting for you at the front door."

She turned onto Hilltop Lane—*Millionaire's Row* in local vernacular. The lawns and rooftops were covered with snow, but the street itself showed little sign of it. Funny how Millionaire's Row and Main Street were always the first ones to be cleared in a snowstorm. Like Tony always said, it pays to have friends in high places. She'd have to remind the maintenance crew where the new president of PMBA resided.

How wonderful that both she and Tony were now in high places here in Port Mariette. Up on Millionaire's Row,

Tony lived side by side with the town's richest people, and his Sweet Treats shop was thriving on Main Street. Rachel had been elevated to president of PMBA, and business at Food 'n Fuel was booming. If only her best friends weren't behaving so strangely right now, her world would be pretty darned perfect.

She made it safely to Tony's, and as promised, he was waiting at the front door, his round belly protruding over his belt.

"I just started a fire for you." He laughed at his innuendo and gave Rachel a hug before nudging her toward the side of the sofa close to the fire. "How was your dinner?"

Rachel slipped off her parka and tossed it on a chair. "I'm not sure. That's why I wanted to talk with you, to get your interpretation."

"Interpretation? You mean tonight was more than just the usual girl talk?"

"Well ... I thought that's what it was going to be, but Suzanne and Marla were both in odd moods. It was like I hardly knew them. Marla was so quiet that at one point, Suzanne actually thought she was having another mini-stroke."

"She wasn't, was she?"

"No. She said she just felt *off* tonight. I don't know what's up with her. It's not like Grace's appendectomy was major surgery or anything."

"Your niece had an appendectomy?"

"Uh-huh. She's fine, but the unexpected surgery is what brought Marla to town. Anyway, she wanted to leave Dom's as soon as she finished her last bite of dinner."

"Marla's always been a mystery, at least to me," Tony said. "I always thought it was bizarre how she showed up for our senior year in high school, then disappeared right after graduation."

She pushed herself from the loveseat and trudged to the front door. She had to put these dark thoughts out of her mind. Grace needed her now. Jesse too. She dared not disappoint.

Opening the door, she forced a welcoming smile. "Hi Jesse. Come on in."

"Hi. How's Grace doing?"

"As far as I can tell, she's doing well, but I just got back. Suzanne and Rachel wanted me to meet them for dinner, and Grace insisted I leave her home alone. I didn't stay long, though, and I brought back some meals for both of you. I'll bring them upstairs in a few minutes."

"Sounds great." Jesse bounded up the steps two at a time.

While microwaving the dinners, Marla mulled over the bizarre experience she'd just had with Suzanne and Rachel. Admittedly, her own strange behavior aggravated the situation, but Suzanne was over the top with anxiety about some sort of homeowner's insurance issue, and Rachel— who was that imperious, unlikeable woman who showed up in her body tonight? Not the Rachel Marla remembered. Rachel had always been the settled one, the reasonable one, the one with hometown values. Now, she sounded more like Marla than Marla ever did. It made Marla cringe to think of how she must have come across to others all those years.

The microwave dinged. She arranged the steaming meals on a tray and carried them up two flights. Outside Grace's bedroom, she could hear her daughter's soft voice.

"Dinner!" Marla announced, although they'd surely heard her footsteps on the creaky wood floor.

"Come on in," Grace called. "Smells delicious."

Like an experienced server, Marla showed them the contents of the tray, and hoped nothing would slide off. She lowered it to a nightstand. "Need anything else?"

'Tis the Time,' Tis the Season

"Suzanne left right away too, remember? She was dying to get out of Port Mariette and travel the world."

"Yeah. Be a stewardess." Tony said it with a little harrumph.

"They call them flight attendants now, you know."

He waved the comment away. "I know."

"And then later on," Rachel said, "she became a trainer for one of the airlines. That job was even more travel—she told me she was gone every week, Monday through Friday. Y'know what, I think she loved all that travel more than she loved people. I never heard from her again until I had to call her about our reunion."

Tony nodded. "Well, at least you three are friends again ... unlikely as that may be." He chortled. "So, what did you girls talk about tonight?"

"Well, we started off talking about Grace's surgery, then Suzanne went on and on about a homeowner's insurance coverage issue. That was as boring as reading the phone book, so when she was finally done, I told them about my PMBA board meeting and Pete's upcoming engagement, and about how he's going to open a new shop."

"Didn't you say anything about me?" Tony flicked his hand on his chest, a look of pretended deflation on his round face.

"Oh, sure. I talked about you a lot. Even told them how you're teaching me to appreciate wine."

"I'll bet they were surprised you switched from beer after all those years."

Rachel tittered. "Suzanne nearly fell out of her chair."

"So, besides homeowner's insurance, what else did your friends talk about?"

"That's my point. They had nothing else to say. It was like eating dinner with strangers. I can't figure it out."

Chapter 10

MARLA

Her coat still on from tonight's dinner, Marla topp[led] onto the mauve-colored loveseat in the foyer of the spa a[nd] dropped her handbag to the floor. *Grace had an abortio[n.]* Such a crushing revelation. Even now, she still couldn[´t] stop thinking about it.

All these years, Grace could have been raising a child— and Marla could have been a grandmother. It was enough to make most women cry.

What a mess she'd been at Dom's this evening. No wonder Suzanne mistook her behavior for another ministroke. *Not a stroke, Suzanne, just a breaking heart.* How could Grace have done such a thing—especially with being adopted herself?

Magnifying the problem, Marla had to acknowledge an awful truth—all those years ago, if she could have figured out a way, she undoubtedly would have done the same thing as Grace. And then Grace never would have been born. Another horrid thought.

Headlights flashed in the spa's front window—Jesse's truck coming up the driveway.

'Tis the Time,' Tis the Season

"Do we have to eat it with our fingers?" Grace laughed.

"Oh, right. Silverware." Marla looked at the tray again. "You need drinks too."

She hurried back downstairs and returned with the missing items. "I even remembered napkins. Need anything else?"

"We're good," said Grace. "Thanks so much." She smiled, making all the effort worth it.

Marla left the room and headed downstairs. Those two needed their privacy—and she needed time to examine the spa's financials without anyone looking over her shoulder.

She clicked open the appointment calendar and tallied the number of appointments by week. The downward trend was quickly obvious. Appointments had begun to dwindle around the time Grace started dating Jesse. Then after they got married, the number of appointments had plummeted.

Unbelievable. At this rate, the spa would not remain a sustainable business. She'd have to infuse it with more cash, but she had already forked over half a million in renovations. She needed to understand the reason why the business was faltering, not just the timeline. Otherwise, what would be the point of propping it up?

It couldn't be Jesse's fault. Surely he wasn't occupying Grace's time. He had a business to run too, and from what she could tell, he seemed to be doing fine financially. The issue had to be something with Grace. But what?

She ought to call Warren about it. While practicing law all those years, he'd dealt with every kind of business issue imaginable. Experience like that could come in handy.

Or maybe that was just her excuse to call him. His note had caught her by surprise. Years ago, before she founded Gemstones Gyms, they'd been in a hot and heavy relationship, but when Warren became her lawyer, he'd nixed anything personal between them. The moment she sold her business, though, he wanted to start things up again. Why not, she'd figured. Of all the men she'd dated, Warren had the most checkmarks on her list of qualities she wanted in a man. Money. Power. Prestige. Smart. Intellectually curious. Socially adept. Physically appealing. Well-educated. The older she got, the harder it was to find all that in one man. Warren was far from perfect, but they had grown into a comfortable relationship, with just the right amount of independence for Marla. She'd hate to lose him.

She plopped onto the loveseat and pressed his number.

Warren answered after a few rings.

"It was a ruptured appendicitis, can you believe it?" She gave him details about the surgery, then added, "Grace needs my help here for a while." May as well be upfront about it, even though Warren always got annoyed when she spent time anywhere without him—especially in Port Mariette. He didn't want to share her with Grace, plus he felt Port Mariette had a bad influence on her thinking. Well, what did he expect? Port Mariette certainly wasn't Manhattan.

"That's fine," Warren said crisply.

"I read your note." She waited for him to comment, but when he didn't, she added, "What's up, Warren? What's on your mind?"

"Nothing I want to talk about right now," he said. "Lots going on. Really busy. I just thought it would be better if we had a pause. I'm, uh, learning as I go with these venture capital investments. For sure, I'm not making any money from it yet."

Not making any money? Or did he mean losing a lot of it? Was he about to ask her for a loan?

Or maybe his VC work was more intricate than she'd realized. Regardless, VCs were not in her wheelhouse.

'Tis the Time, 'Tis the Season

Warren would have to figure things out on his own. "So, you're not upset that I'll be staying here a while, are you?"

"Not at all. It's perfect timing, in fact."

She heard heavy footsteps and dishes rattling. It was Jesse coming down the stairs, attempting to balance the tray of dirty dinnerware.

"I have to go," Marla said. "Maybe we can talk more later." She hung up and took the tray from Jesse.

"Thanks, Marla. That was really good." Jesse smiled. "The silverware and napkins were great too." Jesse ran a hand through his unruly blond curls and pulled on a fleece-lined cap. "I wish Grace could be home with me, but I'm sure she'll get better care being here with you for a while."

Marla gave him a playful pat on the arm. "I'll do my best."

"We're both glad you're here." He grabbed his jacket.

She opened the door for him. As much as she wanted to take care of her daughter, Warren's behavior had shaken her. Staying in Port Mariette could easily be a mistake with undesirable repercussions.

"I'm glad I'm here too," Marla said, not making eye contact as Jesse turned to leave. It had been a very long time since Marla had given thought to the Ten Commandments, but right now, she wondered if she'd broken the one about lying.

Chapter 11

SUZANNE

Suzanne pushed herself away from the tiny desk tucked in the middle of Creations on Main and knocked over a woodcarving. Luckily it was unbreakable. "Ughhh," she growled. "I am so angry." She threw her pen on the desk and stared at Andrea, busy mopping the few squares of linoleum not covered with merchandise. They'd both come in early to catch up on their work, but Suzanne was finding it hard to concentrate in such a tight space. "We are flat out of room here. We have got to find a way to expand."

Her sister kept on cleaning.

Suzanne crossed her legs and bounced her foot.

Andrea glanced at Suzanne's leg and smirked. "There goes that nervous leg again." As opposite as the two sisters were, they knew one another's quirks well.

"Rob says it's important to express our emotions." Although her husband's free advice might irritate her someday down the road, for now, she readily accepted all the help she could get.

Andrea stopped moving but held onto the mop handle. "Believe me, Suzie, I wish we could have gotten one of those vacancies. Either one would have worked out fine for an expansion. But don't worry, something else will turn up."

"If it does, Rachel and her family will scoop it up before we can get to it." Suzanne crossed her arms with a harrumph.

"Let me ask you a question, and don't get mad at me for asking. Might you be overreacting because you're a teensy bit jealous of Rachel? I mean, you and Tony were very tight all through high school."

"Jealous of Rachel? Ha! I don't think so. Haven't you noticed Tony looks a little different now?" She extended her arms in front of tummy to mimic his wide berth. "And how about that fringe he calls hair?" She scoffed. "Besides, I'm a happily married woman now." *Mostly.*

"Okay. I was just asking."

"No, it's not because of Tony." Suzanne furrowed her brow. "I'm mad because we lost out on the chance to expand."

"Are you sure that's all of it? How about that insurance mess with Rob? Could that be what's really bugging you?"

"That's a totally separate issue." Suzanne's chair scraped the floor as she got up. "If I'm being honest, though, I'll admit I am fed up with Rachel—but it's not because of Tony. She's suddenly a different person. Last year, when the three of us got together at our fortieth reunion, we got along so well. It was almost like we were back in high school again. But now, I can't believe how much Rachel has changed, and I don't like it. In fact, I don't like *her.*"

"You want the old Rachel back, is that what you're saying?" Andrea sounded just like Rob.

"Yes. I want my old friend back. She's always been the stable one of the three of us. I want *that* Rachel back."

"Can I make an analogy here?" Andrea leaned the mop against the wall. "Remember how much Mom resisted moving to Sunset Hills? She hated the idea of living in the same building with all those other people. She knew she'd hate the food, hate her room, hate the activities. And look at her now."

"I know where you're going with this."

"Good. Then you know that sometimes people *do* change, even though they say a tiger never changes its spots."

"A leopard, but I get it."

"Well, you got the point." Andrea reached for the mop and continued cleaning.

"Yes, but Mom changed in a good way. The new Rachel? I'm not sure I like her. In fact, I'm sure I don't."

"She'll settle down, just like Mom has. Rachel's going through a lot of changes. Give her a break." Andrea slid her mop closer to the desk. "Imagine how hard it must have been for her to become PMBA president. Then there's her son, Pete. She's gotten used to having him back home with her, and now he's getting married again. Just when Food 'n Fuel has gotten established, Pete wants to open a business for himself. Even Rachel's relationship with Tony is probably stressful. It's hard for a widow to handle dating." She shoved the mop underneath the empty chair. "That's a lot for anyone to take on all at once."

"I get what you're saying," Suzanne said, arms akimbo, "but I still don't agree. Sometimes a woman needs somebody to tell her what she needs to hear."

Chapter 12

RACHEL

Rachel unlocked the back door of Food 'n Fuel as huge fluffy snowflakes floated onto the asphalt and melted on contact. She tiptoed inside and turned on all the lights. Kinda creepy being here all alone. Pete normally opened the place up, but due to his big night out with Lindsey, Rachel had promised to fill in for him this morning.

She busied herself with cleaning counters, restocking shelves, greeting the early morning customers, and taking in local gossip. Around ten, Pete sashayed in, a huge grin lighting up his face.

Rachel clasped her hands together. "Well?"

"She said yes!" He pumped his fist a couple times.

"Hooray!" She grabbed Pete and hugged him. "Was she surprised?"

"Totally."

The front door ding-donged as one of their regulars came in. "Hi, Rachel—hi, Pete," Dr. Hess said, with a little wave of his cane.

"Morning, Doc." Pete tipped the bill of his ballcap. "Been to any good flea markets lately?"

Those two would be talking a while, so Rachel interrupted them. "I'm going to run down to Creations on Main for a minute."

Last night's dinner had been too strange for Rachel's liking. She had to find out what was going on. Surely Suzanne would be straight with her if she asked.

Rachel slipped on her parka and paraded along Main Street's snowy sidewalks, greeting people she'd known all her life. Were they just a little friendlier than they used to be? Seemed like it. In its short existence, PMBA had become influential in Port Mariette, and now, she was its grand poobah.

Straightening her back a little, she admired her posture in the window of Joe's barber shop. Yes, she looked like a leader. Maybe next year she'd run for mayor. After all, Penny had no business being in that role. After all the pain she'd caused the town, she didn't deserve being reappointed to such a powerful position.

Rachel marched on until she reached Creations on Main and saw Suzanne and her sister inside talking with a group of older customers. Local business owners prized these busloads of senior citizens, known for spending wads of money on arts and crafts, antiques, and homemade candy. Sweet Treats was the one stop visitors couldn't resist, and Creations on Main was a close second.

The tinkle of the bell above the door turned all eyes on Rachel. She stood at the entrance and cocked her head toward Suzanne. "Got a minute?"

Andrea shooed Suzanne away. "Go on. I can take care of these ladies myself."

Suzanne stepped toward the door. "What's up?" No warmth in her voice. None at all.

'Tis the Time, 'Tis the Season

Rachel hadn't expected the shop to be overflowing with customers like this. No way could she have a conversation with Suzanne in here. "Uh, how about we take a walk?"

Suzanne grabbed a hooded vest from the desk chair, and they headed outside.

"I wanted to talk with you about last night," Rachel said as they took their first steps along the sidewalk. "Something was different with you and me. Marla too. It's bothering me."

"Okay." Suzanne kept her eyes straight ahead.

"Well, what's going on?" Rachel raised a palm up. "Am I missing something? Did I do something wrong?"

Suzanne shoved her bare hands into her pockets. "Marla and I are both fine. But what's going on with you, that's the question. Last night, you were like a different woman."

"What are you talking about?" Rachel's face contorted.

"Showing up twenty minutes late with no excuse and a weak apology. Drinking wine instead of beer. Do you even realize you talked about yourself all evening? That's not the Rachel I've known since kindergarten."

Rachel gasped. "Look, I've got a full calendar now. I'm running Food 'n Fuel, Pete's getting married, I'm president of PMBA, and on top of that I'm dating Tony—" Rachel put her hands on her hips. "Oh. Is *that* why you're all wound up? You're jealous?"

"Pfft! Jealous? Because you're president of Port Mariette Business Association? I don't think so."

"No—because I'm dating Tony." That had to be the root of Suzanne's anger. She'd never gotten over how he dumped her right before the prom.

"You've got to be kidding." Suzanne eye rolled the comment away.

"Well, then, if not Tony, what is it?"

"You really don't know, do you?" Suzanne narrowed her eyes. "Well, I'll tell you. Did it ever occur to you that others might be interested in those vacant storefronts on Main Street? No, you never gave anyone else a thought. You just took care of your own family. And now, what's the likelihood of something else becoming available anytime soon?"

"That's what you're upset about? Vacant retail space?" This conversation was getting stranger by the second.

"That's at the top of my list."

"Gee, what's the big deal? I was just glad to help Lindsey and Pete get the space they need."

"No kidding. And now, here's me and Rob facing a huge expense for our house in California. I was hoping to expand Creations on Main so I could pay for some of that. But last night, you were too tired to listen to my troubles." She dramatically faked a yawn. "My life is too boring, but everything you're doing is apparently a cause for celebration."

"Oh, boy." Rachel furrowed her brow. "I didn't know you wanted to expand. I'm sorry for taking care of my own family first, but I think if you were in the same situation, you would have done the same."

"No, I wouldn't have." Suzanne said it so loudly that an elderly couple passing by turned and stared.

"Well, there's nothing I can do to fix it now," Rachel said. "It is what it is."

"And I hate how you always said that—*it is what it is*." Suzanne said it in a mocking tone. "What a boring expression."

"I always hated how you talked about all your travels when you worked for the airlines," Rachel spurted. "Like there was something wrong with me because I never went anywhere outside the tri-state area."

"You have to admit, it is rather provincial."

"And I can't stand it when you use words I don't understand. Remember when you were dating that guy who spoke French? That drove me nuts how you repeated everything he said in *francais*. I always felt like you were trying to sound superior."

They turned silent for a moment, then Suzanne said, "Y'know what, maybe we don't have as much in common as we thought, at least not anymore."

Rachel shrugged, pursed her lips.

Suzanne sighed. "The other day I was reading an article about how friends can drift apart as they age. It said sometimes it's best to acknowledge you're different people now and sever the friendship. Life's too short." She looked away.

"If that's the way you feel ..." Rachel's voice drifted off.

"Yes, I do. I'm sorry, but I think it's for the best." Suzanne looked down, then pivoted, leaving Rachel standing alone in the cold.

Chapter 13

MARLA

Marla folded a few paper napkins and placed them on the serving tray, her mind drifting to the peculiar conversation she'd had with Warren last night. Something was up with him, but what? On the phone, the man had a way of skirting any topic he didn't care to address. She longed to fly back to Manhattan to resurrect their suddenly wobbly relationship, but for the time being, leaving Grace was not an option.

She left the kitchen and climbed to the third floor, switching her thoughts to balancing a tray jammed with breakfast options. Surprisingly, the coffee didn't spill, and all the food stayed in place. Triumphant, she arrived outside Grace's half-opened bedroom door.

"Good morning, Grace. How about some breakfast in bed?" Marla said it cheerily, hoping to keep the conversation light today.

"In bed? Oh, my. Come right on in." Grace was still in a flannel nightgown.

Marla lowered the tray to a nightstand, and Grace chuckled at all the options. "Enough for a small army. I hope you're eating some of this too."

"Of course I am." Marla slid a tufted chair next to the bed. "How'd you sleep?"

"Pretty good, considering." Grace reached for a blueberry muffin. "I can't believe you brought me breakfast in bed. I'm not an invalid, you know." Grace smiled, nonetheless, as she took a generous bite.

"Made the muffins myself." A smug look crossed Marla's face, even though the muffins came from a box. She still had to add ingredients and bake them.

"Really yummy." Grace picked up a blueberry from her plate and popped it into her mouth. "Who's scheduled to come in today?"

"Kim Kryzwicki's coming in for a facial at ten," Marla said. "Who's she dating now, anyway?" Rumor was that since her divorce, Kim had tried to make a move on Mitch, as well as other men in town.

"Last I heard, Kim's seeing some guy up in Pittsburgh."

"Good for her." Marla said it half-heartedly. She didn't much care for Kim, who loved to prance about in clothing more suited for a thirty-year-old, like she did last summer when taking golf lessons from Mitch.

Marla continued with the day's lineup. "We've got a few massages this afternoon—and it looks like one of those senior citizen busses must be coming today. Your calendar says something about *August Village* at one o'clock."

"Oh. That's not senior citizens. That's the organization over in Dunham City that helps young people. They do things like foster care, housing, workforce development—all sorts of programs and services, with a focus on youth in transition."

"Youth in transition?" Marla had no idea what that meant, and her face showed it.

"Transitioning out of foster care. They can be in their teens or early twenties."

"Oh. Well, I've never heard of August Village." Marla sounded dismissive and she knew it. She had to get over the belief that everything that matters happened in New York.

Grace wiped the edges of her lips with a napkin. "I'll have to call and cancel them."

"They were coming for manicures, or what?"

"They're not clients. Jesse and I have been volunteering with them. He's hired a couple of them too. Isaiah and Landon."

"Really?" Why hadn't Marla ever heard about any of this before?

"It started with Jesse teaching some of them all the things you'd do in a shop class, like carpentry and basic car maintenance. Then I volunteered to help the older girls with ways to act in a professional setting."

"You'd be perfect at that," Marla said, eager to be positive about anything Grace did.

"The kids aging out of foster care are the ones Jesse and I have been focusing on. They need a lot of help. When they leave the system, that's pretty much the end of any support they get."

"You mean they're out on the street?" Marla found that hard to believe.

"They might get some money through government programs like Medicaid, but not a lot. They have to get a job, of course, but it has to be on a bus line or within walking distance because they don't usually have a car. That obviously limits their options."

Marla wasn't sure where this conversation was headed. "I have to admit, I've never really thought about what happens to foster kids once they're too old to be in the system."

"If Jesse hadn't spent some time in foster care himself, I wouldn't have known much about it, either."

"Jesse was in foster care?"

Grace nodded. "For about a year, when he was in sixth grade." She looked down, shaking her head. "Maybe he'll share the details with you someday. It's his story to tell."

"Of course. If he ever wants to."

"Anyway, Jesse's the one who has given me an education. He says some of these kids have mental health issues like anxiety or depression, and lots of them end up homeless or couch surfing, which is almost as bad. About one in four get arrested for one reason or another. It's tragic. At such a young age, they're abandoned all over again."

"Abandoned. I can understand how that feels." Marla nodded, finally hearing something she could relate to.

"What do you mean?" Grace looked confused. "You were never in foster care, were you?"

Marla wrapped her arms around herself, as if she needed a hug. "No. You know the childhood I had—two parents and every possession I could possibly want, yet I never felt loved. Both of them were too engrossed in their work to notice me." She shrugged. "Certainly not as bad as what you're talking about, but it is a form of abandonment, and it left its mark."

"I never knew things were that hard on you." Grace looked into Marla's eyes, connecting. "I'm so sorry."

"I survived." Marla sloughed Grace's comment off with a shrug. "And I guess these kids do, too, thanks to people like you and Jesse. So, tell me more about August Village."

Chapter 14

SUZANNE

Suzanne walked away from Rachel and went straight into the first shop she saw. Their conversation had been spiraling downward, and she wanted to get away from Rachel before either of them said another word.

Now, Suzanne had to find a reason why she stepped into Hair & Care. It sure wouldn't be for an appointment. Years ago, while covering up the gray in Suzanne's mother's hair, Sharon had accidentally dyed the hair a pale shade of green. By chance, this happened around St. Patrick's Day, so for as long as the hair color lasted, her mother told everyone she was Irish. It beat having her hair stripped and totally recolored.

Sharon, busy on the phone, raised a finger to indicate she'd be off in a minute.

Suzanne glanced at a display case. Should she buy a bottle of shampoo? A new hairbrush? She looked into a nearby mirror, trimmed with holly and pinecones. A nice arrangement, actually. She moved around the salon, taking time to examine all the decorations scattered throughout. Wreaths, stained glass, ceramic Santas, you name it. If only she had the time to make them herself. Creating unique Christmas decorations always lifted her spirits, and in Port Mariette, they always sold well.

After a long minute, Sharon finally hung up. "Well, hello, Miz Cally-for-nye-a," she said, not without some sarcasm.

Suzanne faked a smile at the pronunciation. Did Sharon even have a passport? For sure, Rachel didn't, and whether or not she knew what the word meant, she was definitely *provincial*, and so was Sharon.

Suzanne pursed her lips. She had to lose her attitude. There were worse crimes than being a little provincial—pride among them. *Forgive me, Father.*

"You here to make an appointment?" Sharon readied her fingers above the keyboard.

"Actually, no. I noticed your Christmas decorations as I was walking by and wondered if you'd consider selling them on consignment at my shop. Customers love Christmas decorations. They'll buy them any time of the year."

"Thanks, but they're all gifts from customers. I'd never sell a single one of them."

"I see. Well, it's probably for the best. We don't have enough space for more stock." She leaned forward so no one else could hear. "In fact, I was wondering if you might know any shop owners on Main Street who are planning to close their business for any reason. I'm looking for more space."

Sharon scrunched her aging face in thought. "Other than Mary Frances, I don't know anyone who's leaving, and by now, you probably heard Pete's fiancée is moving in there."

"Pete's fiancée?" Suzanne raised an eyebrow. *My, what a speedy grapevine.* "You're clearly in the know, Sharon.

'Tis the Time,' Tis the Season

I'd appreciate it if you'd call me if you hear of any space opening up."

"You might want to ask Rachel. She hears everything going on with every business in town."

"Good idea. Thanks." Suzanne managed to avoid any hint of sarcasm and slipped out the door.

The rest of the day, she stopped in the shops along Main Street to chat with every owner she could find. Even though no one had plans to leave now, somebody's situation was bound to change one day—and she'd be the first to hear.

Chapter 15

RACHEL

Rachel didn't feel in the mood for much of anything after that conversation with Suzanne, but the sun was out, the temperature had jumped into the forties, and at the moment, not a single customer was around. She'd force herself to put up Food 'n Fuel's Christmas decorations. Even if it didn't lift her spirits, she needed both the exercise and the Vitamin D.

She unearthed a large plastic bin from a storage closet then called into the next room. "Pete, could you help me put up these decorations?"

"In a minute." He yanked a ladder from the closet and met her out front.

As Rachel unraveled the lights, she jerked her chin toward the top of the building. "Good thinking, leaving all those hooks up there last Christmas." That was her Pete, always anticipating the future. She wished she could do a better job of that herself.

He hopped up the ladder then extended his arm toward Rachel. "Ready when you are."

She handed him the end of a string of lights, and her phone rang.

"That's my cousin's ringtone. She never calls just to chat." She held onto the lights as she answered. "Hey, Bernie, what's up?"

"What's up? I should be asking *you*." Bernadette's shrill voice pierced Rachel's ears. "What's going on with your friend Suzanne? She's running up and down Main Street talking to shop owners. She stopped in the bakery and asked me if I'm planning to retire."

"Really?" Suzanne must not have remembered Bernadette was her cousin. "What did you tell her?"

"I told her in the Bible, no one ever retired. Neither will I." Bernadette cackled. "One of these days, I'll fall into a giant bowl of cookie dough and that'll be the end of me. Can't you just imagine it? Sergeant Dan will come by to determine if there was foul play."

"What a great way to go. Maybe I can drop dead eating a ton of chocolate at Sweet Treats." Rachel laughed imagining it, then turned serious. "Suzanne's upset with me because—" She stopped short, not wanting to slip about Esther's pancreatic cancer.

"So, why's Suzanne upset with you?" Bernadette asked.

"A lot of reasons. But underneath it all, I think the real reason she's so unhinged is because of some expensive insurance problem she and Rob are having back in California."

"Oh, I see. Displaced anger. Makes sense. She ought to have a conversation with her psychologist husband instead of tearing around town riling people up. Maybe as president of PMBA, you could try to talk with her."

"Yeah, maybe I could."

Chapter 16

MARLA

"We've been talking nearly an hour, can you believe it?" Marla took a final sip of her coffee, now cold. Grace had given her quite the education, and now it was time for Marla to get moving.

"That was a good breakfast, if I do say so myself." Marla dabbed her lips with a napkin.

Grace chuckled. "I never imagined you making a fancy breakfast like this or taking the time to sit around chatting. It must seem a little peculiar to you, doesn't it?"

"I guess so. But it's nice. Really nice." This time, Marla wasn't breaking that commandment about lying. "I think I might make a habit out of this." She winked at Grace as she reached to place her napkin on the serving tray. "Practically lunchtime now. I'd better clean up the breakfast dishes." She slid the tufted chair back in place by the window.

Grace cleared her throat. "Before you go back downstairs, there's something else I have to discuss with you."

"O-kay." Marla slid the chair back to Grace's bedside. Sitting stiffly, she gave Grace her full attention. What bomb would Grace drop now?

"You know how I told you Jesse and I share the same priorities?" Grace said in a tentative voice.

"Uh-huh."

"Now that we know we can't have a child of our own, we've been talking about where we go from here." She hesitated a moment before blurting out her next words. "We've decided we want to devote ourselves to helping foster kids."

Not sure of what Grace was driving at, Marla chose her response with care. "Well, you're already doing a lot of that with your volunteer work, right?"

"Yes, but we want to do more. Something specific, something with a greater impact."

"Like what?"

"We're thinking of helping those who are aging out of the program. Eighteen to twenty-one, that's the age group that seems best for us. Of course, we're open to other options."

"I see." On the outside, Marla's daughter looked just like her, but on the inside? That was an entirely different matter. Marla couldn't figure her out. "Hmm. Is that why the spa's business has been dwindling, because you've been going down this path for a while?"

Grace grimaced. "I have to confess—my heart's just not in the spa anymore."

Marla struggled to comprehend her daughter's line of thinking. "But you seemed to enjoy it so much, at least when we opened last year."

"Looking back, I think it was more like an adventure I was sharing with you, a way to get to know my birth mother." A smile crossed her face. "You have to admit, that was quite an experience when you showed up and introduced yourself to me. I wanted to know everything about you. But once you left town, and I was on my own at the spa, I lost interest in it." She lifted a shoulder. "The truth is, I've never really been into all that girly stuff."

Grace was right. Marla had never seen her daughter in high heels or with painted nails. Occasionally, Grace might show up in a flowery skirt or a flirty pair of sandals, but that was it. How had Marla been so blind?

She sat still, absorbing Grace's latest revelations. At Gemstones Gyms, she'd learned if an employee wasn't internally motivated, the work wouldn't get done well—or even at all. Even so, she found it hard to believe her own daughter didn't have the same interests and ambition as she had.

"So," Marla asked, patting her thighs, "what exactly would you and Jesse like to do with foster kids?"

"We're not sure yet. There are so many needs. We figure in time, our specific direction will become apparent." Grace took a noticeable breath and let it out. "I didn't want to let you down about the spa, but I figured I'd better tell you how I feel now. That way, you can hire someone to replace me while you're still in town."

"You mean you don't want anything to do with the spa ever again?"

"Well ... yes. That's what I mean." Grace broke eye contact.

Marla's mind raced. She had poured a small fortune into renovating Aunt Adele's neglected home, turning it into a stunning spa, a fun business created just for Grace—and now she wanted nothing to do with it. How could Marla respond in a way that wouldn't offend?

It took her more than a few seconds, but she finally found the words. "I'm sure it was hard for you to tell me this. I'm proud of you for being upfront about your feelings." All Marla truly cared about was her relationship with her daughter. No matter the financial cost, she'd keep that intact.

"Thank you." A weak smile eased across Grace's face. "It seemed like the right time to tell you."

"It'll all work out." Marla wasn't sure how. She said it only because she didn't want to upset Grace.

"Yes, it will," said Grace, her head down. "God has a way of taking care of everything. Even our mistakes."

Marla had made many mistakes in her life, but God had still put Grace in her life. The thought surprisingly choked her up, so she stood. How she hated emotional scenes. "Well, I'm going to go think over what to do about the spa."

She went down the hall to her bedroom and walked straight to the window in the turret. These past two years, she'd spent many hours standing in that same spot. The vista of the river leading to the town always gave her inspiration and a sense of peace.

Even better than the view of Central Park from her condo, she'd always jokingly told Warren.

Maybe there was truth in that, after all.

Chapter 17

SUZANNE

Even though it had been more than forty years since Suzanne had walked into St. Cyprian's Church—this afternoon, it looked surprisingly the same.

Marble floors. Oak pews. Stained glass windows. Carved stations of the cross. The painted plaster statue of Mary. Even the metal box with the slot opening was still there. "For the Poor," read the label on the front. How many coins had she dropped in there over the years?

When she was six, she'd tried to put her allowance in it, but her mother stopped her. "*We* are the poor people they give that money to," she'd whispered as she grabbed Suzanne's hand and pulled her away. It was true. Daddy had left them once again. They were the recipients of the poor box offerings. Such a shameful, scarring revelation.

It drove her to use coupons, buy at thrift shops, and maximize deposits into her 401(k). Even though the airline had let her go before she achieved her retirement goal, she'd come darned close to it, and when she married Rob, she expected her financial picture would improve even more.

After all, he had income from both a successful psychology practice as well as his books and speeches.

Instead, they now faced a massive bill. Where would her share of the money come from? Her retirement account? From Creations on Main? The pressure nearly made her nauseous.

Lately, their phone conversations had been both terse and tense. Would their marriage survive—or was she headed for a second divorce?

And poor Rachel. Suzanne had taken out all her fears and frustrations on her.

Suzanne genuflected and moved into the pew where she used to sit every Sunday. She put down the kneeler and slid onto it. Kneeling—that was something she hadn't done since switching to nondenominational churches. The position felt odd, but still familiar and right. She folded her hands and bowed her head. Tears welled in her eyes.

Forgive me, Father, for I have sinned.

Pouring out her heart, she confessed every sin that came to mind.

In time, she could think of nothing else to say. Her tears had been spent, and at last, she felt at peace. She got up from the pew, genuflected again, and made her way down the aisle.

Before she left, she opened her wallet and emptied it into the poor box.

Chapter 18

RACHEL

"Comfy?" Tony asked Rachel as they nestled together on his soft leather sofa, both in Steelers jerseys, staring expectantly at the ginormous television screen on the living room wall.

"Snug as a bug in a rug." Rachel's head rested on his shoulder.

A basket of potato chips, a bottle of wine, two wineglasses, and two Terrible Towels sat ready on the coffee table. Next to the fireplace, fake icicles shimmered on a real Christmas tree.

On the TV, a ref threw a coin in the air. Steelers won the toss.

"Off to a good start," Tony said, as the game broke for a commercial. "I always like it when they choose to receive."

He pulled his hand from underneath the black-and-gold throw and toyed with Rachel's hair. "I have to admit, I'm kinda glad you decided to let your hair grow back in."

Last summer, Rachel had leaped to the conclusion that Tony was cheating on her, and in a fit of rage, she'd gotten her shoulder-length hair chopped off.

"That pixie cut looked cute on you, but there's nothing like running my fingers through your hair. It's like cornsilk, y'know? The same color, even the same feel."

Rachel smiled contentedly as the defensive players lined up for the first series of downs. "Steel Curtain!" she hollered. She'd learned that from Stan. It was his favorite Steeler callout.

Baltimore's tight end flew into the air, attempting to grab a long pass. A couple Steelers tackled him, and a ref threw a flag. "Face mask, number ninety-two."

Tony jerked to attention. "What do they mean, *face mask*? He hardly touched him!" He growled. "Those refs are blind."

"Calm down. It's only a game."

"Like you've calmed down about Suzanne?" Tony chuckled as he eased himself back on the cushion.

"That's different."

"Different yes, but still a problem. It could cost you the game, if you know what I mean."

"What game?"

"There are lots of games. Business is a game. Life's a game. Even love can be a game." He tickled her in the stomach and nuzzled her neck.

They kissed for a moment, then Rachel pulled back. "So what are you trying to say?"

"In a small town like Port Mariette, you don't want to have an enemy in Suzanne. Even when she goes back to California, her sister Andrea will still be here. I know you think Suzanne was out of line, but she doesn't think so. She's got a lot on her mind right now, and you know how anxious she gets. I used to call her *Nervitis* when we dated. I never knew what would set her off."

"That was back in high school. She's a mature woman now."

"Maybe. But she's not acting like it at the moment. She could cause you problems in your role at PMBA. Look at how she's going around town asking people if they're going to move out. That has ripple effects. Gets people thinking, gets people talking, gets them wondering—*Should I retire? Do I want to have my business here?* You don't want to have a lot of turnover on Main Street. We've got a good thing going here and we don't want to mess it up." He mussed her hair again then kissed her on her forehead. "When someone's an influential person in town like you are, there are repercussions for everything they do."

"I think I see what you're saying." Rachel nodded, taking in his words.

"So just be careful, okay?"

Chapter 19

MARLA

Marla couldn't remember the last time she'd been to a post office. When the clerk told her how much a stamp now cost, she thought he was teasing. People in Port Mariette liked to joke around like that, she'd noticed. In Manhattan, no one had time for such babble.

But the clerk was serious about the price, and the Victorian Spa was out of stamps, so Marla pulled out a credit card and left with three sheets. That ought to last until she figured out what she'd do with the place.

She'd parked her BMW right out front. As she pulled its door open, the stamps slid out of her left hand. She winced. Ever since she had her first mini-stroke a couple years ago, she'd been on the alert for signs of another one. Suzanne knew all about it. That's why she'd leaped to conclusions at Dom's the other night.

Was Marla leaping to conclusions now? She stood still and made a fist. Was her hand tingling, or was it merely her imagination? The sheets of stamps might have simply slipped out. They were a little smooth, after all.

She concentrated on the movement in her body as she bent down and picked up the stamps. All her parts seemed to be working fine. Relieved, she allowed herself a little smile.

"Whoa, there," came a deep voice from a vehicle pulling in next to her. *Mitch.*

She tossed the stamps in her car and closed the door. "Fancy meeting you here."

"*Fancy?*" he retorted. "You making fun of me again?" He jumped out of his truck.

"Only in the nicest possible way." Marla said, stepping a little closer.

"I would expect a woman of your means to pay someone else to run her errands." He smiled at her, the skin around his eyes crinkling. On some people, it made them look old, but on Mitch, it merely made him look rugged, like those tanned cowboys in old cigarette ads.

"Running errands *is* rather beneath me." Joking, she tossed back her mane of shiny hair. "If I'd known you were going to be here, I would have asked you to pick up some stamps for me." She paused. "Hey, switching gears—Do you have time for lunch? I could use some advice."

"Sure. How about Dom's?"

Dom's? She was just there last night. "Why not your country club?"

"Too many eyes, too many ears. Let's go to Dom's."

"Got it." Marla never liked her employees to know her private business, either.

They arrived at Dom's minutes later, greeted at the door by a blow up Santa, an evergreen wildly decorated with too many strands of colorful lights, and the usual opera music playing in the entrance. Understated was not Dom's style.

The hostess led them into the dining room, taking them underneath an arch decked out in fake mistletoe—the spot

'Tis the Time, 'Tis the Season

where Rob had proposed to Suzanne last year. A group of them were together for dinner that night—Suzanne and Rob, Rachel and her widowed neighbor Frank, and Warren had even flown in from New York to be there with Marla.

He'd been so perfect back then.

But now, Warren needed *a pause* in their relationship. Her shoulders drooped at the thought.

Mitch stood at the table, waiting for her to sit first. Physically, she took her seat, but her mind still dwelt on Warren.

A server interrupted her thoughts. Marla asked for a small Caesar salad.

"No appetite?" Mitch raised an eyebrow.

"I had a big meal here last night. I have to do penance today."

"You should have told me." Mitch ran his eyes over her. "You hardly need to punish yourself, but we could've had a slice of veggie pizza at Herbie's instead. Now *that's* a private place," he said in jest. Herbie's Pizza had lousy acoustics, and the tables practically touched one another.

Mitch leaned back in his chair. "So, what's on your mind?"

One of the things she appreciated about Mitch was what he called his no-baloney rule. If he had something to say, he didn't need to write a note about it, he just said it, and said it plainly.

She was tempted to tell him about Warren wanting to take a break. Maybe a man like Mitch who knew her well could offer some helpful insight.

But no. She'd tell him about the spa. That was her immediate concern. Mitch would be the ideal sounding board for that.

"What did you want to discuss?" Mitch repeated.

"The spa," Marla blurted. "I don't know what to do about it. Ever since Grace got involved with Jesse, it's been losing money."

He waved the comment away. "Ah, they've been married only a few months. Maybe she's been spending a lot of time with him. I've heard that's what newlyweds do."

Marla ignored Mitch's banter. "Has Jesse said anything to you about the spa?"

"No." Mitch wasn't one for gossip. "But even if he had, you know I might not be able to talk about it." His eyes twinkled. "Don't worry, he hasn't said a word to me. I promise."

"Sometimes I wonder if Jesse's a good influence on her."

"Look," Mitch said, leaning toward her, now serious. "You know I met Jesse when I was doing prison ministry down in West Virginia. Trust me, you don't have to worry about him. He's a changed man now. Sometimes, the guys who fall hardest and get back up end up being the best men of all."

"He could easily relapse. Do you know if he goes to NA meetings or therapy or anything like that?"

"He goes to NA meetings."

"How can you be sure?"

Mitch heaved a sigh. "Look, Marla, there are few secrets here in Port Mariette. Jesse goes to NA meetings. Can't you just trust me? You know I'd never lie to you."

But Warren might. She'd seen some of the crafty moves he'd made as her lawyer.

The server arrived with their meals. Mitch bowed his head, ready to say the blessing.

Marla stared at him as he prayed. How did he come up with such perfect words? Why did he seem so comfortable praying out loud? She could barely eke out a few sentences silently, and here was Mitch rambling on about all sorts of topics, making it sound like every word came from his heart. How did he do that? Maybe someday she'd ask him. He finished the prayer by asking God for clarity about the spa, and Marla said *amen* along with him.

As they put their napkins on their laps, she looked at Mitch's chicken parm sandwich, red sauce oozing from all sides, and wondered how he'd get out of here without a stain on his sweater.

Mitch swallowed his first mouthful. "What does Warren think you should do about the spa?"

"I don't know." She poked at her salad. "He hasn't commented."

"A lawyer without an opinion? That's a first."

Marla stabbed a cherry tomato with the fork. "The fact is, Warren told me he needed a *pause* in our relationship. Actually he didn't tell me that. He wrote it in a note he stuck in my carryon before I caught my flight here." She brought the tomato to her lips.

"A *pause*." Mitch stared at her lips, opening to accept the tomato. "How about that. Very lawyerly of him to use a word that's open to interpretation." Mitch massaged his chin. "And to write it down so he didn't have to explain what he meant by it."

"Exactly." Marla leaned toward Mitch, spreading both hands on the tablecloth. "I hate when he does that."

"Mighty strong word, hate." He glanced at Marla, as if gauging her reaction. "Words come from the heart, you know."

"I know. I just don't need his aggravation right now."

They ate in silence for a moment, then Mitch leaned back in his chair again. "I have a feeling there's something else on that beautiful mind of yours."

She looked across the table and stared at Mitch. Why were the ends of his mouth curling into a small smile? There was nothing pleasant about today's lunch topics.

"Well ..." Marla hedged a moment, then decided to unload it all. "Grace admitted she doesn't have much interest in running the spa. In fact, she said she'd rather do something with foster kids, can you believe it? What a curveball." Marla ran a finger along the rim of her water glass. "I may not agree with her plans, but I'm going to support her in whatever she's passionate about. I have the means to do it, so why not?"

"And why do you want to support Grace's dreams with your money?" He stared at her. "You know you can't buy love."

"I know that. But between me living in Manhattan and her now being married, I hardly ever see her. The way I look at it, if my wealth enables her to realize her dream, I know she'll appreciate it." Marla pressed her hands together in front of her lips, almost like she was praying. "And over time, maybe it will help us grow closer. Like a real mother and daughter."

"Well, it's a start." Mitch said. "What did you have in mind in terms of helping her?"

"I'm thinking of turning the spa into apartments for young people who have aged out of foster care."

Mitch let out a soft whistle. "That's quite the undertaking."

"It's the most logical solution, don't you agree?"

He rubbed the side of his neck a few times. "I guess you could do that, but is it logical? I don't know about that. I imagine you'll get pushback from some people in town. There are a lot of building codes you'd have to abide by too. Off the top of my head, I'd say you'd have to add some bathrooms, a fire alarm system, and an emergency staircase on the side of the building. Plus, you'd want to change the décor, and you have a lot of fancy furniture you'd have to get rid of."

"An emergency stairwell on the side of the house would look so ugly." Marla sank in her seat. "That house is absolutely beautiful."

"Thank you," Mitch teased. Marla may have paid for the renovations, but Mitch and his team had done all the physical work.

Marla didn't even hear him. Her mind was occupied with visualizing the changes. "It would be a shame to mess that house up. Maybe we could put the fire escape on the back."

"You'd have to talk to the building codes guy, Fred Nettles. He can be a stickler about the oddest details. I'm sure there would be other roadblocks to overcome too, like rental property or zoning regulations. I have no idea. You'd have to do some digging." He winked and his eyes once again formed those happy crinkles on both sides of his face. "Maybe even some praying."

Marla rolled her eyes, but in her heart, she knew he was right.

Chapter 20

SUZANNE

Toting a Christmas wreath she'd made for her mother, Suzanne hurried through a snow squall and burst into the foyer of Sunset Hills. She signed in and waved to Penny, who waved back but didn't look up. Ever since Suzanne had volunteered Rob to provide mandated therapy for Penny, she avoided eye contact with Suzanne. A pity. Throughout all the messes Penny got herself into, Suzanne had been her chief and sometimes only advocate. What was wrong with that woman? Did she think Suzanne listened in on her therapy sessions with Rob? Or that he repeated to her anything Penny said?

One thing Suzanne did know—Penny must have been challenging to work with. After he'd finished her last session, he admitted he was glad they were done. He'd never said that about anyone else.

Suzanne left the foyer and raced past the dining room. It still smelled like dinner. Stuffed cabbage rolls or sauerkraut, she couldn't tell which, but either way, her nose was offended. With as few inhales as possible, she made it to her mother's room. The door was wide open, and inside, her mother was rocking and reading, her usual evening activity. Suzanne cleared a space on the end table next to her and put the wreath on it.

"Such nice handiwork," her mother said, fingering the pine cones. " Did you make it yourself?"

Suzanne nodded. "I got the idea from something I saw at Hair & Care."

Her mother looked up, appalled. "You didn't get your hair done there, did you?"

"No, of course not." Suzanne shook her head. "It's a long story, but I had to stop in there." She motioned toward the wreath. "You ought to recognize everything on there. It's all from your front yard. The pine cones are from those evergreens next to the driveway, and these are some branches from your holly bushes."

"I remember when I could make things like that." Her mother opened her hands as much as she could, but they were nowhere near flat. "Now, I can barely get myself dressed."

What could Suzanne say? "Maybe your fingers will feel better if the weather warms up like they're predicting." In this part of Pennsylvania, a brief stretch of temperatures in the fifties or even sixties did sometimes occur in December.

"I think I need hot temperatures, not warm ones. Summer's a long way off." She eyed the wreath again. "Do you think there's a chance you'll be staying until Christmas?"

"It all depends on what happens with Rob's house."

"I was wondering ... is the house still in his name only?"

"Actually, he had the deed changed to both our names after we got married."

"That's so like Rob, always thinking of the other person." She rocked a few times. "Of course, that means you're both liable for all those expenses now too."

'Tis the Time, 'Tis the Season

"I know." Suzanne squirmed.

"But that's what marriage is all about, sharing the good and the bad."

"Yeah, for richer or for poorer." Suzanne said it with a roll of her eyes.

"I'm glad you finally settled down with Rob. He's a wonderful husband."

A wonderful husband who hadn't even purchased proper insurance for a cliffside home. *What was he thinking?* But no point complaining to her mother about Rob. In her eyes, he could do no wrong.

"Yes, Rob's a wonderful husband, he's a man of integrity, and I love him to bits," Suzanne said. "He's just not so great with details. Like insurance." She scrunched her lips.

"Oh, honey, stop worrying. You and Rob will figure it out."

"But it's going to cost us a fortune," Suzanne whined. "We have to pay for all that work ourselves."

"It's only money, Suzanne. You can both earn more. Don't let this situation ruin your marriage." Her mouth curved into a smile. "Do you remember that old Buick we had when you were little?"

"The one where Daddy forgot to change the oil?" They'd been driving home from visiting relatives when white smoke streamed out underneath the hood like a volcano erupting. Her father hadn't bothered to change the oil in ages. The engine was ruined, and the car had to be junked. "You bet I remember. Who could forget that story?"

Her mother nodded. "You know your dad and I had trouble in our marriage. Some of it was because I had a habit of criticizing him."

"Seriously, Mom?" They both knew he was a gambler and a philanderer. Why would her mother take even a drop of the blame?

"No one's perfect, Suzanne." She gave her daughter a sideways glance, then flicked her wrist. "Anyway, we were sitting on the side of the road waiting for a tow truck, and I was steaming like that Buick. I took a good look at your dad. The expression on his face was like something I'd never seen—a mixture of anger, embarrassment, and fear. I knew if I said a word, he'd go over the edge.

"The tow truck came, and somehow we made it home. We had to junk the Buick and buy a new car. His carelessness cost us a pretty penny, and money was tight. I never said a word then or anytime later. He felt bad enough and didn't need me harping about it."

The sun now low on the horizon, her mother gazed out the window, where the hydrangea bushes she loved had been trimmed to stubs. "Those were the days, weren't they?" She shook her head, a nostalgic look on her face.

Suzanne nodded but couldn't bring herself to smile. Her mother's story about the Buick brought back memories of sitting in the back seat that day, terrified of what their father might do. Like her mother, Suzanne had kept quiet too. Even then, she knew her mouth could get her into trouble.

Her mother touched the wreath. "Could you hang this on the door? I think there's a hook on the front."

Suzanne picked up the wreath and hung it. "Thanks for the story." She hugged her mother goodbye and drifted down the hall. First chance she had, she would apologize to Rob for the things she'd said. Then, to Rachel.

Chapter 21

RACHEL

Rachel jammed a saucer into the bottom rack of the dishwasher and loaded detergent in the wash compartment.

"If you've got any dirty dishes out there, bring 'em in here now," she hollered to Pete, watching TV in the living room. "I'm running the dishwasher."

Cinders, her black lab mix, clicked across the kitchen's linoleum floor. He whined, then pushed his bowl with his big nose.

"Okay, Cinders, I got your hint." She poured some fresh dog food into the bowl and refreshed his water.

Pete quickly appeared with a coffee mug, a fork, and a dessert plate. He shoved them willy-nilly into the machine.

Rachel rearranged them and pressed the start button. She stretched her arms wide and let out a loud yawn. "Boy, am I tired today. They should schedule weeknight football games earlier in the evening."

"I went to bed at the half," Pete said. "Didn't even hear you come in." Pete plopped onto a seat at the kitchen table, a sheet of paper in his hand. "Any chance you've got enough energy to look over this guest list Lindsey and I put together? I want to make sure we don't forget anyone."

Normally she wouldn't have cared who he invited to his wedding, but as PMBA president, she had to be politically astute. This was just the thing Tony had been warning her about. It wouldn't do well if even one significant person was overlooked.

She took a seat and pointed to the end of the table. "Could you hand me those reading glasses? Lindsey's handwriting is so tiny." In fact, everyone's writing seemed smaller these days.

"When did you get reading glasses?" Pete picked them up and examined them. "Purple frames?" Grinning, he handed them to her.

"I picked them up at the drugstore last week. They're a big help with fine print." She put them on. "What do you think?"

"I think they're what they call *statement eyewear*." Pete's eyes twinkled as he teased her.

"What kind of statement do you think I'm making?"

"Don't mess with this lady."

"Hm." Rachel tipped her head. "Then, obviously, I picked the right ones." She laughed, then dropped her eyes to the list.

"See anyone you think we can cut?" Pete asked.

"Lemme look." Rachel perused the list quickly, saying *good, good* as she called out a few names. Her finger stopped about three-quarters of the way down. "Who are these four people?"

"Lindsey's cousins," Pete said. "They live somewhere in New England."

"If you've got to make a cut, they might be the ones to go." She continued down the list. "Suzanne? Oh, boy, I don't know about that one."

"What d'ya mean? She's one of your besties." He chuckled, apparently amused at his word choice.

"Not anymore."

"Look," Pete said, "I know Suzanne's miffed about not getting one of the vacant shops, but by the time the wedding rolls around, all this will have blown over."

"Maybe." Rachel squinted as she contemplated the situation. Suddenly, she brightened. "Your wedding is months away. Suzanne will be back in California by then."

"So, leave her off the list?"

"Nah, keep her on it. She'll say she can't afford to fly in from California. You'll still get a nice gift—and I can say I'm the bigger person."

She couldn't wait to tell Tony how well she was learning to play the game.

Chapter 22

MARLA

Marla stomped the rock salt off her Gucci boots in the foyer of Sunset Hills. How she disliked winter. Already dark outside, and it wasn't even six o'clock. On top of that, ice, snow, and cold temperatures. Technically, winter hadn't even begun yet. Three more months of this misery.

At the reception desk, she jangled the pen on its chain to catch the attention of Penny, gabbing on the phone. If there was one person Marla needed on her side right now, it would be the beady-eyed mayor of Port Mariette.

Penny turned and hung up as soon as she saw Marla. "Hi. I heard you were in town again." She stepped closer to the registration pad to talk.

Marla nodded. "And I heard you're mayor again. Lucky you."

"Yeah, I'm such a lucky gal." Penny said it sarcastically. "Being mayor only pays a few thousand a year—with no health insurance, can you believe it? So I need this job too."

"Makes sense." Marla wasn't about to question the woman's career choices. With a history like hers, she was lucky indeed to have both jobs.

"You're here to see your aunt, I presume?"

Marla nodded. "I stopped in the other day for a quick hello. Didn't see you anywhere. Maybe it was your day off."

"Day off? Not a chance. I'm here every day, for at least a few hours. But I run around a lot, checking up on this and that. I must have missed you."

Marla dropped her voice so people passing by couldn't hear. "I could be wrong, but it seemed like Aunt Adele's hearing is getting worse. Maybe I was hurrying her or talking too fast. Have you noticed anything?"

"I don't know about that, but—" Penny dropped her voice as well—"She seems to be slipping a little. Mentally." She tapped the top of her head. "I could be wrong too. See what you think."

When Marla first came to town for her fortieth reunion, her aunt had been showing mental lapses, like calling her *Marlee* instead of *Marla*. At Sunset Hills, though, she seemed to rebound. At least until now.

"I'll check it out. Thanks for telling me." Marla walked away from Penny just as Suzanne came around the corner on her way out.

"One in, one out," Marla said, a smile on her face. "How's your mom doing?"

"Pretty good." Suzanne glanced at Penny, busy at her desk. "Got a minute?" She motioned for Marla to take a seat on the far side of the foyer.

"What's up?" Marla said, crossing her long legs.

Suzanne wrung her hands as she relayed the conversation she'd had with Rachel yesterday. "I think it was the right thing to do, but I wish I hadn't been so harsh. What do you think?"

"Don't be so hard on yourself. You're under a lot of stress right now, and let's face it, it's not easy to keep a friendship going after all these years. People do change over time. At least you were kind enough to tell her directly instead of ghosting her like an immature teenager. If I were you, I'd be upset over losing out on those vacancies on Main Street too."

"I just feel really crappy about it now. Friends are hard to come by at our age."

"Maybe you'll find a way to smooth things over. I hope you can." Marla stood, signaling she was done with their conversation. The last thing she wanted was to get caught in the middle between Rachel and Suzanne—especially with Rachel now being PMBA president.

"Grace is home alone," Marla explained. "I'm stopping in to see Aunt Adele for just a few minutes. How about we talk again later?"

After a quick hug, they separated. Marla went down the hall and found her aunt asleep in an easy chair, lightly snoring, her mouth an open slit. Gently, Marla kissed her on the forehead. "Good evening, favorite aunt."

Aunt Adele shut her mouth and opened her rheumy eyes. "You're back again so soon? How nice."

"I was hoping we could talk about a few things."

"Okay, but you'll have to speak up. My ears have been bothering me lately. Maybe I've got some wax in there. Do you think you could arrange to take me to an ear doctor while you're in town?"

"I'd be glad to," Marla said loudly as she took a nearby seat.

"So what's on your mind?" Aunt Adele pushed a button on her chair and brought herself upright. She always got straight to the point. Just like Mitch. Marla loved that about her.

"I'd like to talk with you about Grace."

"Grace?" Aunt Adele cocked her tiny head. "She's not having any complications from that appendix surgery, is she?"

"No, she's doing fine. But she told me something surprising—she claims she's lost interest in running the spa."

"That's strange."

"She now wants to get involved some way in the foster care system."

"Ahhh." Aunt Adele nodded a few times. "She's finally losing her life to save it."

Her aunt wasn't making any sense. Was Penny right about Aunt Adele's mental state?

"Out of the blue, Grace told me she and Jesse want to get involved with young people aging out of foster care. She said they want to *devote* themselves to young people."

"*Devote*? Did you say *devote*?"

"Yes, *devote*." Marla repeated it a little louder.

"That's a mighty strong word."

"I thought so too," Marla said.

"But it doesn't surprise me." Aunt Adele smiled as if she knew more about the situation than Marla. "Grace has such a soft heart, and God wants to use her. So, what's next?" Aunt Adele raised what was left of her eyebrows.

"I want to help her."

"You're not going to throw money at her, are you? You know that's not the way to get her love."

"I know, I know. You sound just like Mitch." Marla patted her aunt's veiny hand. "I was thinking we could convert the spa into an apartment building for young people who've aged out of the foster care system. Mitch says it would be a huge undertaking, so before I move forward with anything I wanted to get your blessing."

'Tis the Time, 'Tis the Season

Aunt Adele smiled, shaking her head. "You don't need any blessing from me. When I moved into Sunset Hills, I turned the house and all that land over to you. I know you'll do the right thing. You have a good mind, just like your mother and dad. How are they doing, by the way?"

Marla managed to contain her reaction. Both her parents had died in the past year. Aunt Adele hadn't made it to the funerals, but Marla had definitely told her about their passings.

"Can't say," she finally blurted. "I haven't talked with either of them recently. Have you?"

"No, I haven't either." Aunt Adele looked up to the ceiling, as if searching for a lost thought. "How's your man friend, by the way?"

Another question that would be difficult to answer.

"Warren?" Marla snorted. "He said he needs a *pause* in our relationship."

"A what? Can you speak up a little louder?"

"Warren wants a *pause* in our relationship." Marla practically screamed the word.

"A *pause*? What's that all about?" Her aunt turned up the volume. "I thought you two would be married by now."

"I wish." Marla imagined being married to Warren, sitting next to the windows in his living room. Or maybe they'd live in her condo instead. Lately, he seemed to prefer her place to his. That would be fine by her. She had the better view and wouldn't have to pack a thing. He'd be poring over his legal papers, and she'd be reading the *Wall Street Journal*, calling out items of interest to him.

"I just remembered something." Marla jerked her chin. "I forgot to suspend my subscription."

"To what?" Aunt Adele's face looked confused.

"A newspaper. It just dawned on me that Warren won't be picking up my *Wall Street Journal*. I need to call them about that."

"Your life is so complex, Marla. I don't know how you keep everything straight."

"I don't, either." She sighed.

"Well, William's a nice man. I hope he comes to his senses."

William? Marla thought back to when Aunt Adele had sometimes gotten confused about Marla's name. Why was she suddenly regressing? Should she correct her or just let it be?

She put her hand over her aunt's. "It's Warren, not William."

"Oh, right." Aunt Adele closed her eyes tightly, as if committing Warren's name to memory. "Names are so hard to remember these days. Warren, Warren, Warren. There. I'll remember his name now. Nice man." She tilted her head in thought. "Mitch is a nice man too."

"Mitch thinks highly of you too, Aunt Adele."

"What does he think of your plans for the spa?"

"He's intrigued, but a little negative about the idea."

"I guess that's understandable." Aunt Adele nodded. "With all his contracting experience, he's seen it all—both good and bad."

"He said to expect a lot of obstacles along the way, and any one of them could ruin our plans."

"Take it one step at a time. You're in no rush, right?"

"Actually, after Grace's health scare, I do feel a sense of urgency."

Aunt Adele patted Marla's hand. "I like your plan to put the house to good use. Let God guide you with everything. He'll tell you what to do every step of the way."

'Tis the Time, 'Tis the Season

Marla leaned toward her aunt and kissed her on the cheek. "Thanks. Love you." She left the room and headed to the front desk, where Penny's chair now sat empty.

As she signed out, Penny returned, a little breathless.

"Oh, I thought you'd already left for the day." Marla put the pen down.

"Pit stop before going home." Penny grinned as if it were a highlight of her day. "How's your aunt?"

"I'd like to talk with the facility doctor about her. Could you ask someone to give me a call?"

Penny officiously picked up a pen and jotted herself a note. "Will do," she said, with that stupid grin still pasted on her tiny face.

Chapter 23

SUZANNE

Suzanne's GPS said she had plenty of time to get to her daughter's house north of Pittsburgh, but she knew driving straight through the city on a weekday morning, unexpected traffic jams could pop up. A grandmother should never be late for her only grandchild's first birthday party, so Suzanne pressed the doorbell—although in hindsight, she probably should have parked a few blocks away and waited a half hour or so.

"She's here already!" Suzanne could hear Jill inside, calling to Drew. The rest of their words were indistinguishable, probably for the better.

Eventually, Jill answered the door, her hair tied in a loose topknot, and balancing the baby on her hip. "Hi, Mom." Jill's smile looked genuine but stressed.

This frenzy was not Suzanne's fault. It was her daughter's idea to have the party in the morning when Drew would be working from home and could pull away for an hour or so.

Suzanne stepped inside, laden with gifts.

"Why don't you put them on the sofa," Jill said.

After arranging them, Suzanne took the baby from Jill's arms. "Happy first birthday!" Suzanne made excited faces at her.

Elizabeth let out a squeal of appreciation, apparently not seeing anything wrong with Suzanne's silliness or early arrival.

Suzanne lifted the baby high in the air. "Whee!" They both shrieked with delight. Did life get any better than this?

"Careful, Mom." Jill raised a hand. "You might drop her."

"I used to do that with you all the time," Suzanne said. "I never once dropped you."

"Maybe so, but you were a lot younger then."

"I still have good muscle tone. That's what my GP said at my last wellness visit." Suzanne cuddled the baby. "And you, sweet Elizabeth—you will grow up strong and healthy too."

Silently, she said a birthday blessing for her granddaughter. Both Jill and her husband Drew were *not into religion*, as they repeatedly reminded her. Never mind that praying itself was not religion. To keep the peace, she'd stopped praying aloud, but they couldn't stop her from praying silently. Or whispering into Elizabeth's ear when they weren't around.

"I'm so glad you were able to come for her first birthday. I never dreamed you'd be in town." Jill took the baby from Suzanne's arms. "Drew's on a call. He'll be down in a minute. We can open the gifts then."

Drew worked in finance, but Suzanne still had no idea what he actually did, other than make gobs of money. The house they'd built had amenities Suzanne had never even heard of. Jill had to show her how to use the warming drawer, and the automatic lighting in the pantry still startled her every time she opened the door. As for the cold plunge tub, well, that was simply insane, although Jill said Drew swore by it. If Suzanne ever took one of those ice baths, she'd swear *in* it.

"Hi, Suzanne." Drew bounced down the steps in flashy jogging shoes. Long ago, she'd asked him to call her Mom, but he'd continued to use her first name. It wasn't as if his own mother would get jealous—the woman lived in Australia. Chances of overlapping visits were quite slim.

Suzanne gave Drew a hug, barely returned. "How are you?" she said, knowing the answer.

"Great."

He always said that.

"Come see the cake, Mom." Jill placed it in the middle of their elegant but highly impractical glass dining room table. "The icing is Elizabeth's favorite color."

How Jill could know a one-year-old's favorite color was beyond Suzanne, but she could play along. "My, what a pretty shade of purple you've chosen, Elizabeth."

After Drew lit the lone candle, they sang *Happy Birthday* several times, as Jill required multiple takes in order to achieve video footage worthy of social media. No one really minded, though. Especially Suzanne. Living in California, how often would she get to sing that song to her grandchild in person?

Eventually, they moved into the living room, where Elizabeth was set free to attack her gifts. Boxes, bows, wrapping paper, and gift bags flew everywhere.

Once everything had been opened, Jill separated the gifts from Suzanne into two piles—safe and unsafe. At least the safe pile was larger than the unsafe one. Next time, she'd have to get more suggestions in advance.

Drew glanced out the front window, then put on a hoodie. "I think I'll go out for a run before the snow hits." He sped out the door.

"He sure loves his running." Jill smiled and shook her head.

"That's nice, how you don't mind he ran out the door in the middle of the birthday party."

Jill smiled. "He's not avoiding the party, Mom. He's just giving you and me some time to talk. Isn't that thoughtful of him?"

"Oh. Yes, so thoughtful." *Men.* Would she ever figure them out?

"Drew's such a good husband. A wonderful father too." She scooped up the baby and gave her a kiss. "Daddy loves you, doesn't he?" Jill purred. "Don't get me wrong, he's not perfect, but neither am I, and he never bugs me about anything. So I try not to bug him, either."

"Looks like it's working well." Another reminder, by contrast, of how poorly she'd been treating Rob the last few days.

Jill came closer and lowered her voice, as if sharing a secret. "You know I've been telling Drew I wanted another baby."

Suzanne nodded. Jill had talked about it a lot in their phone conversations.

A huge grin spread across Jill's face and her eyes sparkled.

Suzanne knew that look. "You're pregnant!" Her hands flew up in excitement.

"Yes!" Jill touched her tummy and nodded with vigor. "I just took the test yesterday."

"Oh, my gosh, what great news!" Suzanne wrapped her arms around her daughter. They joyously rocked back forth, as Elizabeth laughed at their nonsensical behavior.

"Now you'll have to fly back for visits even more often," Jill said.

'Tis the Time, 'Tis the Season

"For sure I will." Suzanne said the words with confidence, yet she wondered how she would ever afford the extra tickets. *Instead of flying, maybe I'll have to walk.*

Chapter 24

RACHEL

Rachel was filling Food 'n Fuel's refrigerated cases with the latest batch of pierogies when Walt Celinski sauntered in the door.

"You must have ESP, Walt. I just stocked up on your favorite."

He walked over and took a bag from her hands. "Cheese and potato filling. Yep, that's my favorite." He grabbed a few more. "Rosemarie will be happy too. Just heat and serve."

Rachel slipped the sacks of pierogies inside a thin plastic bag. "So what's new in your world?" As the owners of the *Port Mariette Gazette*, Walt and Rosemarie had lots of influence. Now more than ever, Rachel needed to stay on their good side.

"What's new? Our oldest son Christian will graduate this semester. He finished early."

Of course. The kid was brilliant.

"What's he planning to do with himself?" Rachel didn't even know what Christian's major was, much less his career plans.

"He's been working at the newspaper off and on since he was twelve," Walt said. "We've been grooming him to take over the business. Now, Rosemarie and I will have some time for traveling before we get too old to enjoy it."

Traveling. Why were people always wanting to get away? Wasn't home good enough for them?

"Where will you go?"

"I want to go to Williamsburg, and Rosemarie wants to go see that life-size Noah's Ark in Kentucky. We don't want to stray too far away from home. Gotta keep tabs on the business."

"Yeah, I know what you mean. Pete does a good job, but sometimes we don't see eye to eye on how things should be done. I tell him, until I'm dead and buried, I get final say on how we operate Food 'n Fuel." Rachel laughed, knowing there was more than a little truth to what she'd said.

"Christian thinks we should move our advertising office from Main Street. Put it with the printing plant, he says. I keep trying to tell him people want their newspaper to have a presence in the town. They like to stop by, chat, place an advertisement. That's how we pick up a lot of our stories. But you know how young people are, full of ideas." He shook his head. "Just not necessarily better ones."

"I can relate." Only yesterday, Pete had talked with her about rearranging the shelves, claiming it would increase sales if they put their most profitable items at eye level. She had a hard enough time doing inventory already and didn't need to learn new locations for every item.

"By the way, Walt—if you decide to move, you might want to give me a heads-up. I usually know who's on the lookout for space." A scoop like that might get her back in Suzanne's good graces.

"Will do." Walt nodded as he glanced around. "Christian thinks we need to do more investigative reporting too."

'Tis the Time,' Tis the Season

"Like what?" Rachel wondered what could possibly be worth investigating in Port Mariette.

Walt hesitated.

Pete, the only one in the store, was leaning over the counter doing something on his phone. Probably a social media post. A waste of time, in Rachel's estimation, but Pete claimed it was good for business. How could she prove him wrong? She knew nothing about social media and didn't care to learn.

"I wanted to get your opinion on something." Walt reached in his pocket for a pen and notepad.

"My opinion? About what?"

"I've heard some rumors, and I'd like your input. As PMBA president, I'm sure you've heard about the change at the spa."

"At the spa?" She couldn't imagine what Marla and Grace were up to. Why hadn't they shared their plans with her?

A customer walked in the door and greeted Pete.

Rachel motioned to Walt. "Why don't we go back to my office so we can talk in privacy?"

Chapter 25

MARLA

For once, the spa was busy. What a fluke. Hannah had four facials scheduled, Latoya was booked solid with massages, and the phone kept ringing. All morning, Marla hadn't had time for anything but a cup of coffee. At noon, Grace came downstairs and insisted on relieving Marla for a lunch break.

Gobbling a sandwich in the kitchen, Marla could see her daughter juggling clients and phone calls with ease. Clearly, Grace could manage the business well. Too bad she lacked the desire to do so, but at least her skills would be useful when they converted the spa into apartments.

Marla couldn't wait for the right moment to share her big idea with Grace, but first, she wanted to prepare some drawings. The spa was huge, and its space could be rearranged in several ways, depending on whether occupants were singles who had aged out of the system or possibly foster families that need affordable housing. If necessary, she could always ask Mitch to knock out some walls. In such a large house, the possibilities seemed endless.

She would give up her bedroom on the third floor too. Even though she'd miss that view of the river, she'd do anything to help Grace realize her dream. Maybe Grace would ask her to stay with her and Jesse the next time she came to town. What a bonus that would be.

The activity in the spa suddenly quieted down. Grace popped into the kitchen for a drink.

"I could have brought you something," Marla said, finishing the last mouthful of her sandwich. "It never occurred to me you might be thirsty."

"Not to worry." Grace reached inside the refrigerator. "Remember, I'm not an invalid. I can get my own drink."

"I'm done eating, but before you go back upstairs, can you give me a minute to make a quick call?" Marla dialed a number, then pressed a few more times to reach a human being.

"I'd like to cancel my subscription," Marla said to the *Wall Street Journal* customer service rep.

"You're sure? I see you've been with us for more than twenty years."

"Yes. Cancel it, please." Marla had no idea when she'd return to Manhattan, and Warren definitely wouldn't be picking up her newspapers anytime soon.

"Instead of cancelling, maybe you'd rather suspend your subscription? That way, when you want to start getting the paper again, it's just a simple call instead of having to go through the sign-up process."

"Good idea. Let's just suspend indefinitely."

She ended the call and looked over at Grace resting against the kitchen counter. "I can take over now. I want you to relax the rest of the day."

"Is that an order?" Grace tipped her head.

"Definitely an order."

"Okay, I relent." Grace rolled her eyes, but Marla knew she was just kidding.

'Tis the Time,' Tis the Season

"I think I'll take a long shower and maybe a nap." Grace yawned as she stretched her arms high. "Jesse's stopping over later with a pizza for an early dinner." She put her glass into the dishwasher. "Thanks for filling in for me."

A shrill voice from the front desk surprised them. "Yoo-hoo. Grace? Marla? Are you back there?"

It was Penny, ready to pay for her pedicure. She'd wandered downstairs noiselessly in her bare feet, pink foam separators between her toes.

Grace followed Marla to the front desk, where Penny pointed to her bony little feet, grinning. "I asked for a Christmas look." Her toenails were half green, half red, with sparkles on top.

"Oh, I love the look!" Grace sounded like she meant it.

Marla thought they looked absurd, especially on a woman Penny's age, but who can understand taste? Or maybe now that Mary Frances had moved to Florida, Penny was trying to lure Herbie back into her clutches. Would her oddly decorated toes succeed? Who knows. Marla had met plenty of men in Manhattan with weird fetishes. Maybe Herbie's was toes.

Despite her true opinion, Marla followed Grace's lead and gushed over the pedicure. "So festive. Perfect for the season."

"Aren't you getting your fingernails painted today too?" Grace asked. "It would look so nice if everything matched."

"Hands, I can do by myself. Toes, they're a lot harder. All that bending and stretching. Besides, I have to get back to work." She paid her bill, slipped on her flip-flops, and paraded out.

Marla and Grace controlled their laughter until the door closed behind her.

Chapter 26

SUZANNE

"Bye-bye, birthday girl," Suzanne blew one final kiss to her granddaughter and toppled into her car exhausted. If she ever had the chance to babysit Elizabeth, how would she manage? Apparently she'd have to put her to bed very, very early.

Backing out of the driveway, Suzanne called Rob. "I've got some great news."

"Great news? I could use some of that." Rob sounded like he needed an ear, but for the moment, all she wanted to discuss was her happy news.

She gave him details of the party and finished off her monologue with the news of Jill's pregnancy. "Isn't that fabulous?"

"Yes. Soon, you'll have two grandkids." Rob sighed. "I'll still have none." Rob's son lived with his girlfriend, with no plans to marry—much less have a family, and his daughter cared about nothing except her fast-track career.

"Don't be sad." Suzanne said it softly, hoping to console her husband. "Now that we're married, they're your grandkids too."

"Technically, I guess you're right, but it's just not the same."

It took a lot to get Rob down, and judging by the sound of his voice, he'd hit his limit. Should she apologize now for how upset she'd been with him over the house? Maybe that would lift his spirits. She considered the idea but passed on it. Apologizing over the phone didn't seem right.

Instead, she sweetly asked him for an update. "How are things going with the house? Everything moving along okay?" Suzanne hadn't intended to make a pun and wondered if Rob had even noticed.

"Dirty. Noisy. Expensive. Aggravating. I'm trying to do some writing, and I'm getting nowhere." Never had she heard him sound so disgusted.

"I wish I could do something to help."

"Me too."

Suzanne brightened. "Hey, babe, I just got an idea. My mom's house is pretty barren right now, but there's plenty of room for the two of us. Why don't you come to Port Mariette for a while? I miss you so much. It's quiet here, so you'd be able to concentrate on writing, and I think if we were together, we could come up with a plan to pay for all those repairs. Even if we couldn't, I'd feel better about the situation just being with you."

Rob paused for a few long seconds. Suzanne's heart beat a little faster as she waited for his response. She could hear him tapping on a computer. Was he going to spring another surprise on her?

"I'm online right now. There's a flight that lands tomorrow around six in the morning. Would you mind driving to the airport that early?"

"To pick up my husband? Whom I love? Who wants to be with me? You know I'll be there, honey. Can't wait!"

Chapter 27

RACHEL

Rachel continued restocking inventory after Walt left. The more she thought about their conversation, the more her irritation grew.

Feeling ready to burst, she stormed down to Sweet Treats, all the way to the other end of Main Street. The place was empty, except for an artificial Christmas tree decorated with candy canes and fake sugarplums.

Tony was probably making candy in the back room. Judging by the pounds he'd put on since opening his shop, Rachel estimated he ate about a tenth of whatever he produced.

She'd struggled with her weight too, having had a sugar addiction of her own as long as she could remember. Lately, she'd learned a trick to become more disciplined. Every time she was tempted to buy something sweet at the Dairy Mart, she'd say a *Hail Mary*. Usually, it stopped her from buying things she shouldn't, and except for an occasional pierogi, she could usually control herself from eating whatever was in the refrigerator. Right now, though, that walnut fudge in Tony's refrigerated display case sure looked tempting.

"Tony, are you back there?" She sounded a little shrill, but this was urgent.

He emerged from behind the curtain, wiping his hands on a black apron. "Hey, sweetie, what's up? Your cheeks are so red—is it that cold outside?"

"No. It's only around forty degrees. I'm not cold—I'm hot."

Tony stepped around the counter. "That's my girl. Hot, never cold." He pulled her closer to him.

She pushed him away. "Not that kind of hot. I'm hot under the collar."

"How come? Suzanne bugging you again?"

"No. Worse than that. Walt just stopped by. He asked me if I'd heard about the spa being turned into a home for foster kids. Can you believe it?"

"Seriously?"

"Can you imagine the impact something like that would have on this town?" Rachel had never met anyone from August Village, but she'd heard plenty of stories. Nothing but trouble.

"Have you talked with Marla about it?"

"She never mentioned a thing about it at dinner the other night."

"How about Grace?" Tony asked. "Have you talked with her?"

"Grace and I haven't talked since her surgery." Rachel pursed her lips. "Besides, Grace only manages the spa. It's Marla who owns the mansion and all those acres that go with it."

"Maybe Marla didn't want you to know about it," Tony said.

"Or maybe she doesn't want PMBA members to know." Rachel thrust her hands on her hips. "A change like that is bound to get a lot of business owners riled up. Guess who will be expected to deal with it—me."

Chapter 28

MARLA

Last night, having nothing else to do besides watching inane TV shows, Marla had drifted off to sleep early, and now, she found herself wide awake well before the sun rose. She put on a robe, pondered life for a while, then padded downstairs for coffee. In a noiseless place like Port Mariette, this kind of quiet was an experience to savor.

While the coffee was brewing, she unlocked the front door and reached into the fresh snow to retrieve the day's *Port Mariette Gazette*. A far cry from the *Wall Street Journal*, but the paper did provide her with light entertainment.

Like the day Esther's checkbook was stolen. Front page news. An outraged Penny was certain someone passing through town had snatched it from Esther's antique shop. The whole town was in an uproar. Then the next day, readers learned Esther had found the missing checkbook under her bed, where it must have fallen when she changed the sheets.

Marla slid the paper from its plastic sleeve and settled into a chair next to the fireplace, prepared to start the day with another amusing small-town story.

The front-page headline jerked her to attention—*Foster Care Housing May Be Coming to Port Mariette*. Her mouth dropped open as she absorbed the article, inaccuracies and all.

How could they print such a story? She hadn't even run the idea by Grace yet. Who was the paper's unnamed source? Obviously, Grace couldn't have told a soul. Aunt Adele probably heard only half of what Marla had told her. Could it have been Rachel? There were several comments attributed to her, all of them speculation, nothing concrete. Penny? She only admitted to hearing rumors. Fred, the building codes guy, was quoted as saying he knew nothing about the plans—the only true statement in the entire article.

That left Mitch. He would never reveal her plans, would he?

She smacked the paper down on the table. Why the heck hadn't Walt Celinski called her before printing this? What shoddy journalism—if she could even elevate his rag enough to call it that.

She reached for her phone.

A missed call from Warren? She hadn't heard it come in. She flipped the phone to its side. Still turned off from last night. She shook her head at her forgetfulness. Is this how the long slide started with Aunt Adele, a careless mistake here and there? Or maybe she simply had too much on her mind.

She called Warren back first. He could probably suggest some kind of legal action against the paper.

"Hi, Marla." He sounded neutral, like a lawyer greeting a client.

"You called?" She responded, defensiveness in her voice.

"Yes. Thanks for calling back."

'Tis the Time, 'Tis the Season

He didn't sound like he was calling to hear about her day, so before bringing up the newspaper article, she waited for him to say whatever was on his mind.

"Uh ... look," Warren finally said. "I know I told you I needed some time, a pause in our relationship."

"And?" She tensed her body. Would he say he'd had enough of a break, or that he needed more time alone—or something else?

"Well, there's no easy way to say this, Marla. I think we've hit the end of our road."

"*The end of our road?*" She wrinkled her forehead, something she always tried to avoid. It took such a toll on facial skin. "What are you talking about?"

He paused a moment before continuing. "I don't like being second on anyone's list. Ever since you connected with Grace, she's been your top priority. I don't expect that will ever change, do you?"

She couldn't argue with him about that. Grace would always take first place in her life. But losing Warren over that? No. She'd have to figure out a way to fix this.

"I hear what you're saying, but we can figure out a way to make it work." She sounded like a businesswoman, not his romantic partner, and he sounded like he had her on a witness stand. Hard to break habits learned over so many years.

"It's not just that." Warren let out a long sigh.

Just then, a floorboard creaked somewhere upstairs. At this hour, it had to be Grace.

"Grace is on her way downstairs," Marla whispered. "I can't talk about this right now."

"See what I'm talking about? Grace appears, and you're ready to hang up on me."

"I'm sorry, Warren. I can't talk now. We'll have to continue this conversation later." She had never complained when he took client calls. Why couldn't he understand?

She put the phone down and hid the newspaper inside a drawer. "Good morning." Marla put on a smile.

Grace appeared on the landing, scowling. "Aunt Sissy just called me." She tromped down the rest of the steps.

For a fleeting second, Marla thought Rachel might have called to inquire about her recovery, but Grace's footsteps said otherwise. Marla slowly opened the drawer. "Is this what Rachel called you about?" She held up the paper.

"Yes." She snatched it from Marla's hand and strode to the velvet loveseat where she read in silence.

Marla managed to keep quiet until the spa's business line rang. She forced another smile and answered the call politely. A cancellation for this afternoon, no, not interested in rescheduling. Marla didn't bother trying to change the client's mind. What would be the point?

Throughout the call, Grace glared at Marla. The moment Marla hung up, she said, "Why would you do this to me?"

"I'm not doing anything *to* you, Grace. I'm doing it *for* you. Don't you see?"

"I never asked you to run my life or make my career decisions. Not for me, and certainly not for Jesse."

"I was waiting for the right time to tell you about the idea." Marla pulled another drawer open. "I've been working on the drawings." Carrying them to the loveseat, she sat close to Grace. "Please don't be upset with me. I had to talk with Mitch first to see if the idea was feasible, then I reviewed the plan with Aunt Adele. Even though she turned this house and all the property over to me, I thought it was only right to talk with her before moving ahead."

Grace, her jaw set, didn't say a word.

"Aunt Adele loved the idea, by the way."

"Who else did you tell?"

"No one. Not Suzanne, not Rachel, not Warren. No one else."

"Well, obviously someone talked to Walt at the paper." Grace looked at the front page again and shook her head. "I can't believe you made plans for me and Jesse without even discussing it with us. What were you thinking?"

"To be honest, I thought it was a terrific idea." Marla had expected appreciation for her idea, not anger. Could the surgery have affected Grace's hormones? Possibly. But no matter, Grace was still angry. "I guess I was wrong." Marla looked into Grace's weary eyes. "I'm sorry. Very sorry."

Grace turned her head away and let out a disgusted sigh.

All this, and the sun's not even up. Marla considered going back to bed. Maybe life would look better around ten a.m.

Grace pushed herself up and walked toward the stairs. "I have to talk with Jesse about this." She took a few steps and stopped. "In the meantime, why don't you try to find out who leaked the story?"

"Will do."

Mitch or Aunt Adele. It had to be one of them. Aunt Adele had kept Marla's secrets all those years. It had to be Mitch. But why would he do such a thing?

Chapter 29

SUZANNE

Suzanne wasn't ready to open her eyes yet. She loved floating in the dreamy space between half-asleep and half-awake. Her mother's old mattress might have been a little lumpy, but as soon as she and Rob got home from the airport, they'd made the most of it. With Rob not being able to sleep on his flight, and Suzanne emotionally exhausted, small wonder they'd drifted off into a morning nap.

Rolling to her side, her hand brushed against Rob's back. He stirred and stretched.

She climbed on top of him and nuzzled his neck. "Hello, sleepyhead."

He wrapped an arm around her and ran his fingers through her wavy hair. "Hello, beautiful." He kissed her forehead, then her earlobe, then her neck.

"Coffee, tea, or me?" She said it in a husky, suggestive voice. The line had been a standard one back in the days when she worked as a stewardess. She never dreamed at her age she'd be saying it to her beloved husband. Funny how God works.

Rob ran his hand down her back. "Hmm. Let me start with you, and we can work our way into coffee later."

"Honey, before that, I've got something to say."

Rob's brow furrowed.

"I'm ... I'm sorry I've been such a jerk about all this insurance stuff." Finally, she had found the words she'd been wanting to say.

Rob placed his index finger on her lips and smiled. "Apology accepted. Now, no more talking." He cupped her face with his hands and gave her another kiss, as if he'd forgotten every mean word she'd said to him these past few days.

What a husband. What a blessing. What a wonderful life they shared.

A little later, dressed in jeans and T-shirts, they sat together at the kitchen table sipping coffee, glancing at each other in the way newlyweds of any age do, their eyes sparkling and faces glowing.

Rob finished his coffee and walked to the kitchen counter. He stretched and yawned then looked around the room. "Seems to me like your mom's house could use a little help from a man. Loose doorknobs, a dripping faucet, and cold air coming through the caulking around the windows." He put his cup inside the dishwasher and closed the door. "Those are the kinds of issues that ought to be fixed before you put this house up for sale."

"I agree," Suzanne said, "but I don't know if we should spend money on a handyman right now."

"Here's a surprise for you," Rob said. "I'm a bit handy myself. As long as I'm here, I can make a few repairs. Even minor improvements can have a noticeable impact on the sales price."

Suzanne put down her cup and stood. "The toolbox is in the basement. I'll get it for you." She scurried down the steps and returned with a large metal box. "It was my dad's."

"Looks brand new."

'Tis the Time, 'Tis the Season

"I don't think it got a lot of use."

They spent the next couple hours working around the house, all the while discussing their financial situation. The distraction of their tasks somehow made it easier to talk things through.

Sometimes Suzanne felt like raising her voice, or saying something she knew she'd regret, but she managed to control herself. What was the point of yelling? They'd eventually find a way out of this mess—although at the moment, neither of them knew how.

Chapter 30

RACHEL

Rachel's phone didn't stop ringing all morning, and only a few of the calls related to food orders. The rest were business owners ranting about the newspaper article. She even got a few visits.

Sharon from Hair & Care stopped by first to spew her venom. "This is not going to happen in my town, and certainly not in my backyard." Sharon, whose preferred state of being was anger, lived relatively close to the spa, although her house was separated from it by several acres of wooded land.

"I know, I know." Rachel spoke in a soothing voice, like she used to do with her boys when they were fighting over the TV remote. "It's a problem. I'm going to call Marla and find out what's going on."

"You've got to do something to stop it—before it's too late. After all, isn't that what the president of Port Mariette Business Association is supposed to do? We're counting on you to protect our interests, and if you can't, you should resign."

Resign? Rachel would never admit defeat, even when up against Marla.

Sharon finally left, then one after another, irritated business owners called or stopped by to complain. Although none of them were as confrontational as Sharon, Rachel could see she had to take action fast.

She grabbed her jacket and said to Pete, "This is getting out of hand. I've got to go talk with Marla."

"Before you leave, could you give Lindsey a call? She's afraid the change at the spa will affect residential sales. With the opening of her second office here on Main Street, the timing couldn't be worse. She's all worked up. Can you calm her down for me?"

"Sure. I'll give her a call on my way to Marla's." Lindsey was a sweetie pie, but her Chicken Little tendencies got on Rachel's nerves.

"Would you mind calling her now, before you leave?"

"Why can't I just call her while I'm driving?" Lindsey might be a new member of PMBA, but she was only one of several dozen Rachel had to satisfy.

"If you call her now, I can repeat the same message when I see her tonight. Maybe both of us giving her the same message will convince her to ease up. She's really whacked out over this."

Rachel held in a sigh. "Sure." She wanted to keep her future daughter-in-law happy—besides, it gave her a reason to delay a difficult conversation with Marla. "Lindsey's probably all jittery with the wedding coming up, isn't she?"

"Probably." Pete shrugged as he looked away.

Chapter 31

MARLA

Now that Grace had stomped back upstairs, Marla pushed away from the spa's front desk and walked over to the wide front window. The sun's rays peeked through the rows of pines along the driveway, pillows of snow resting on their branches. A few deer pranced across the front lawn, leaving a path of hoofprints in their wake. The scene looked like it belonged on an inspirational greeting card.

Moved, Marla took in a deep breath then exhaled a prayer. "*Oh, God,*" she whispered, "*you know I want to have a good relationship with my daughter. I'm trying as hard as I can, but I've made a mess of it. I need your help.*"

Was it enough? The right words? Would it work? She had no idea. She should have paid better attention to the nuns.

She turned back to the desk and dialed the *Port Mariette Gazette*. She got Walt's voicemail. Could he be avoiding her call?

She texted Mitch next. *Can I stop by? I need to talk with you.* She paced, waiting for his reply. Confrontation in business never bothered her, but this was personal. Very personal.

To her dismay, Mitch took a couple minutes to reply. Was he avoiding her too?

Leaving for a job site. If you can come over now, I'll wait 4 U.

In seconds, she was out the door and in her car, then minutes later at Mitch's. She slammed her car door shut and strode toward the side door.

Mitch was waiting for her, his jacket already on and a folded newspaper tucked under his arm. He pulled it out. "Is this why you're in such a huff?"

"You bet." She spat it out.

"C'mon inside. Let's not get the neighbors talking. Might create another gossipy headline tomorrow."

She marched down the hall to his office then turned to face him. "Grace is furious with me."

"Doesn't she like your idea?"

Marla jabbed the paper. "This is the first she's heard of it. She said she doesn't want me running her life. Or Jesse's. On top of that, I'm getting angry calls from people I don't even know."

"And why are you so angry with me?" He crossed his arms. "It's not my fault."

"It had to be you who leaked this story." She poked his arm.

"Hey." He grabbed her finger and didn't let go. "That's a pretty big presumption on your part."

"Well, it certainly wasn't my aunt, and you're the only other person I talked to about this plan." She tried to pull her finger free, but he held it tight.

"I didn't tell anyone anything. Why would I do a cockamamie thing like that? Maybe you should go talk with Adele." Finally, he let go of her hand.

She turned away. "No matter who spilled the story, Grace is livid." She choked up. "All I've been trying to do is be helpful to her, to have a good relationship with her, and now she's furious with me."

Mitch put his hands on Marla's shoulders then lifted her chin with the tips of his fingers. A long lock of her hair had fallen over one of her eyes. He smoothed it back then touched her cheek with a rough hand. "Marla, you know I'd never do anything to hurt you. Why don't you go talk with your aunt." He let go of her.

She touched the side of her face. For some reason, she couldn't think of what to say.

"I have to go," he said, motioning toward his office door.

She wobbled down the hall in front of him, then drifted into her car. Mitch wouldn't lie. It couldn't have been him. That leaves Aunt Adele. She must be slipping more than Marla realized.

On the way to Sunset Hills, her conversation with Mitch kept running through her head—and so did Mitch's tender touch with his rough hand. All the time they'd spent together these past two years, their physical contact had been limited to bumping shoulders in a golf cart or passing the salt at Dom's. Today was the most intimate interaction she'd experienced with him, and it had her rattled.

Arriving at Sunset Hills, she found a distant parking space and hurried inside. With gray clouds looming above, she'd probably be trudging through snow on her way out.

At the reception desk, Penny leaped like an attack dog from her office chair. "What's going on at the spa?" She waved her copy of the newspaper. "I'm the mayor, remember? You should be discussing something like this with me first. When Walt asked me about the rumor, I didn't know what to say. I looked like an out-of-touch fool."

"Look, I don't know how the story got in the papers. I'm ... I'm not sure myself what's going on. I need time to think."

"Good idea. Take a pause."

Chapter 32

SUZANNE

Suzanne massaged Rob's muscled shoulder while he tightened a doorknob screw. "I know you've only been in town a few hours, but I was wondering if you'd like to use some of your handyman skills at Creations on Main?"

"Nothing would please me more." Rob grabbed Suzanne playfully, then planted a kiss on her lips. "What needs to be done over there?"

"I was wondering if you could put a few more shelves on the walls."

"Do you already have the wood? And the brackets?"

"I do." She'd been planning to do it herself, but surely Rob would do a better job. "If you want to do it today, I'm supposed to open up at eleven."

Rob tossed the screwdriver into the toolbox.

"If you have the time, that is." She tenderly touched his unshaved face.

"I'll be ready in a minute." He took the stairs two at a time while Suzanne packed the trunk.

They were soon on Main Street and slipped into a parking space near the shop. While they unloaded the trunk, Sharon from Hair & Care flagged them down. "What the heck is your friend Marla up to?" She shoved a copy of the *Port Mariette Gazette* an inch in front of Suzanne's face.

Suzanne stepped back. "I don't know what you're talking about."

Rob reached for the paper and held it up so he and Suzanne could see the first page. They read for a few seconds then exchanged confused looks.

"I don't know a thing about this." Suzanne spoke gently, not wanting to stir Sharon up anywhere near Creations on Main. Could be bad for business.

Sharon grabbed the paper from Rob's hands. "You can tell your friend one thing from me—Not in my backyard!" She thrust her hands on her hips. "NIMBY!" She pivoted away.

"Where can we get a copy of that paper?" Rob asked.

Suzanne pointed at the mail slot and unlocked the front door. Inside, she grabbed the paper and read it aloud dramatically, like she used to do when reading the plane's safety instructions all those years ago. When she finished, she said, "I'm shocked Marla didn't say anything about this to me."

"Or Rachel," Rob said. "It sounds like she was one of the sources. You'd think she would have mentioned it to you too."

Suzanne squirmed. "Well, that I can explain." She told him about her recent disagreement with her.

"Hmm." Rob nodded a few times. He said nothing, just looked at her without judgment. One of so many reasons she loved him.

Even so, she knew she'd made a mistake blowing up at Rachel, and Rob's silence had just confirmed it. "I know I have to fix that situation with Rachel, but I want to talk with Marla first." She'd figure out what to do about Rachel later.

Chapter 33

RACHEL

Pete huddled nearby while Rachel spent ten minutes on the phone quelling Lindsey's fears. "You're quite welcome, Lindsey," Rachel finally said, trying to sound like she meant it. "Call me if you have any other questions." She disconnected the call and turned away from Pete so he wouldn't see her rolling her eyes. He was going to have his hands full with this one.

"Thanks a lot, Mom." Pete left her to take care of a customer waiting at the counter.

Rachel put her phone down, and someone outside wearing red caught her eye.

Unbelievable. Only a few feet away, Marla was pumping her own gas. Or at least attempting to. Smart as that woman was, Rachel watched her stand there for what seemed like at least a full minute reading the instructions on the pump.

Rachel couldn't help herself. She kept gawking at Marla, pumping gas in a red quilted jacket with a fur collar.

She had hoped to confront Marla anywhere but on her own business property, however, *carpe diem* was what the nuns had preached in Latin class, so she pushed the door wide open and strode toward the gas pumps.

Marla looked up from the side of her BMW and glared at Rachel.

Rachel winced.

Maybe if she began with something useful. "Need help with the pump?" Rachel immediately realized her question was pointless—the numbers on the pump were now spinning.

"I'm good." Marla fixed her eyes on the pump as she continued filling her tank.

"Got a minute to talk? In my office?" Rachel jerked her chin toward the entrance to her commercial kitchen.

"When I'm done here."

Rachel went back inside and moved a few piles around on her cluttered desk as she sat waiting. What should she say to Marla? How should she say it? She didn't want to lose a second friend, that much she knew. She bounced her heels on the floor, trying to remove the tension she felt all over.

As soon as Marla strode inside, Rachel blurted, "I didn't tell Walt anything." May as well get right to the point, that's what Marla liked. "His questions caught me off guard, but the idea did sound like something you would dream up. You always think big, and I know you'd do anything for Grace."

Marla dropped down onto the chair next to Rachel's desk. "I know you didn't tell him anything about the spa plans. But why did you have to say you knew it would bring *nothing but trouble*? That's such an inflammatory statement, and you have no basis for saying that."

Rachel steeled herself. After all, she was PMBA president and had to behave like it. She'd speak in that soothing voice she'd just used on Lindsey.

"Look, Marla, Port Mariette is a small town, the kind of place where people have lived for generations. We don't

'Tis the Time,' Tis the Season

want a lot of strangers moving into town. A family here and there, fine. We've got to keep the population growing. But these young people you're hoping to bring here, who knows what their upbringing was like? What kind of education did they get? Do they even go to church?"

Marla stood. "You have no idea what you're talking about, and I'm not going to argue about something that is only in the preliminary stages."

She walked toward the door then turned to face Rachel again. "I just remembered a story I read a while ago. Apparently a couple of homeless guys started sleeping at night on the lawn of a church. They weren't bothering anyone, just sleeping there. People in the congregation noticed them and began complaining—who are these people sleeping on our church's lawn? After a few days, the man who was in charge of the church's homeless ministry came outside and told them they had to leave. He said they weren't allowed to sleep on church property." She shook her head. "Is that what Port Mariette's like? A bunch of churchgoing hypocrites?"

Marla was out the door before Rachel could come up with a response.

Rachel pursed her lips, tapped her pen on a tablet, then picked up her phone.

"When can we talk?" she said to Penny.

Chapter 34

MARLA

After her distressing conversation with Rachel, Marla returned to the spa. Stomping her boots on the foyer's oriental rug, she noticed some chunks of rock salt on it, undoubtedly eating away at the fibers.

Rock salt wasn't something she wanted to touch with her manicured fingers. Searching for a vacuum cleaner, she opened some closets and found a stick-like device hanging from the wall. No cord and a tiny dust bin. What a marvelous invention. Did her cleaning woman back in Manhattan know about this?

As the machine hummed, her mind roamed. Who did Aunt Adele tell about the plans for the spa? Did she even remember telling anyone? No matter what her aunt had done, Marla would never get angry with her. Aunt Adele had opened her home to Marla when she was pregnant, arranged for the baby's adoption, and tolerated her all through her miserable senior year at St. Cyprian's Academy. The woman was a saint. Marla didn't need any Pope to tell her that.

Marla vacuumed her way up to the third floor. On her nightstand, Warren's note caught her eye. She owed Mr. Venture Capital a call.

She closed the door and picked up her phone. "Do you have time to talk?"

"You finally decided to call me back." Warren answered, irritation in his voice.

"Sorry. There's a lot going on here." She recapped the newspaper story and her conversations with Penny and Rachel.

At the end, he let out a sigh.

"Is that all you have to say—a sigh?"

He sighed again, louder this time. "I'm sorry you're having some issues, but I've got issues of my own."

"Like what?" Before she'd left for Port Mariette, other than being a little stressed over his venture capital deals, he hadn't even hinted at any problems. What else could be bothering him?

He cleared his throat. "Do you remember that couple down the hall from me, Lucas and Yolanda, from Brazil?"

"Vaguely."

"Lucas is the one who got me interested in VC deals. I spent a lot of time at his place talking with him about his investments. I got to know him and his wife pretty well."

"Okay, so what's the point?" Sounded to her like he might be hitting her up for money.

"They're, uh, getting divorced."

"Oh. That's too bad." Yet another reason why she'd avoided marriage. She didn't want to end up being a divorce statistic.

"And I've ... I've been seeing Yolanda."

"What?" Marla choked. She tried to speak, but nothing else came out.

'Tis the Time, 'Tis the Season

"I'm sorry, Marla. I thought it would just be a fling. I wasn't even going to tell you, but now ..."

"You weren't even going to tell me?" She could feel her anger rising as she stiffened all over.

"It didn't seem to have legs at first, you know what I mean? But after a while, well ..." He stopped talking.

"And now you're off and running on those legs." She blew out a puff of heated air. "Okay." She took a moment to consider the implications. For sure, she'd never be able to trust him again. "I'll be hiring another lawyer for the foundation, obviously."

"I understand." Warren said it like he expected the change.

"And I'll stop by to pick up a few things I have at your place. When I'm back in Manhattan, that is. Whenever that will be."

"Or I can drop them off. Everything's already boxed up."

Already boxed up? How oblivious could she have been? "Sure. Leave the key with the doorman." She sounded like a robot.

"I'm sorry it's ending this way," Warren said, just as robotically. "Maybe someday we'll be able to be friends again."

Still in shock, she didn't know what else to say. Was it over for sure? In the years Warren was her lawyer at Gemstones Gyms, he'd had more than a few flings. Maybe Yolanda was just his latest. His interest could pass quickly. No matter. She'd never trust him again. Not personally, not professionally.

Numbly, she said goodbye then collapsed onto her bed, emotionally exhausted. She closed her eyes and forced herself to focus on breathing slowly, deeply. Her body relaxed and she drifted off.

A knock on her door wrecked a dream she'd been enjoying, the details of which she immediately forgot. How long had she been asleep?

"Are you okay in there?" It was Grace's voice.

Marla pushed herself up and opened the door. "I was taking a little nap," she said, wishing she could have stayed in dreamland. Real life was so much harder.

"Are you feeling all right?" Still standing at the doorway, Grace raised an eyebrow, concern written across her face. Had her anger about the newspaper article subsided? Or was she actually worried about Marla?

"Thanks for checking on me," Marla said. "I'm fine, but I've got to run over to see Aunt Adele. I'll be back before any clients are due." She grabbed the stick vacuum and hurried down the steps before Grace could respond, then drove to Sunset Hills and zipped through the halls to her aunt's room.

"Hey there, beautiful," Marla said as she entered.

"You again?" Aunt Adele turned the TV off.

Marla took a seat beside her. "Have you seen today's paper?" She showed her the front page. "I'm mystified." Marla tried her best to sound perplexed. "Do you have any idea who might have told Walt about my plans for the spa?"

"I don't have a clue." Aunt Adele furrowed her brow and looked up, perhaps seeking an answer in the plasterboard ceiling tiles.

In the hallway, an aide chattered as she went by with someone in a wheelchair. A moment later, Penny passed by, her eyebrows furrowing at the sight of the newspaper in Marla's lap.

Marla squinted in thought as Penny quickly disappeared down the hall.

A pause. Penny had said the word *pause* to Marla. Who uses that word in everyday conversation? No one. In Port

Mariette, they might say *take a breather* or *take a break*, not *take a pause*.

She got up and closed the door. Returning to her seat, she whispered to her aunt. "Something just dawned on me. I think I know the source now." She nodded a few times as she considered her revelation. "Lots of eyes and ears here at Sunset Hills."

"Oh, yes." Aunt Adele waved a hand, as if the statement were obvious to anyone. "Last night, I could hear Janet across the hall. She had gas again." Aunt Adele tittered, then lifted her chin toward a wall. "And Bob next door, he snores a lot."

Janet has gas.

Bob snores.

And Penny has big ears.

Someone knocked at the door.

"Time for meds?" Marla asked her aunt.

"I don't think so."

"I'll see who it is." Marla got up and opened the door.

"Could I talk with you in the hall for a moment, Marla?" Penny's birdlike head seemed to be shaking.

You bet you can. Marla stepped into the hall, her jaw set for confrontation.

"I have a confession to make," Penny blurted.

Marla crossed her arms and squeezed them against her ribcage to prevent her from verbally expressing her anger—one of many tricks she'd learned in her years of dealing with irritating clients.

"I'm listening," she said through her teeth.

"I, uh, happened to overhear you talking with your aunt the other day about your plans for the spa." Penny squirmed, then looked at Marla with pleading eyes. "You know how I feel about strangers in Port Mariette. I'm sure you remember how I fought the new highway exit."

"Of course I do." Penny's excuses for trying to block an exit for Port Mariette last year included her fear that the *wrong kind of people* would come to town.

"So when I heard what you were up to, I kind of panicked again."

"In other words, you lump anyone who grew up in foster care with thieves, drug dealers, and drunk drivers."

Penny winced. "I just want Port Mariette to stay the same. I want it to stay safe. That's why I told Walt I'd heard a rumor. I thought if he printed something about it, there'd be such an uproar you wouldn't move ahead with the idea."

"You don't know me very well, Penny. If anything, it's having the opposite effect on me." Marla put a hand on her hip. "I'm curious, though. Why are you admitting you leaked this to the paper?"

"Well ... you probably know I had to agree to get counseling with Suzanne's husband, after I wrote all those anonymous bad reviews about local businesses, right?"

"Of course." Marla had attended the meeting where that was decided.

"In my sessions with Rob, he said dishonesty is like weaving a spider web. Eventually, you get caught in your own lies. That's what happened to me last time, and when I saw you holding that newspaper, I realized I was bound to get caught again. I don't want be fired as mayor a second time." Penny heaved a sigh. "So, I have to tell you the whole truth."

Marla tapped her toe a few times but kept her mouth tightly closed, waiting for the rest of Penny's story.

"The other day when we were talking at the front desk, I accidentally said something about taking a pause because I had overheard you saying that to your aunt. Obviously, I heard about you talking about your plan for the spa too.

'Tis the Time,' Tis the Season

I realized once you read the story in the paper, sooner or later, you'd put two and two together."

"I did figure it out—but only after I wrongly accused an innocent person."

"You accused someone else?" Penny brightened, as if Marla's pain lessened her own. "Well, I guess you'll have to fess up now too."

Penny was right about that. Marla would have to apologize to Mitch. In the few days since her arrival, she'd apologized to Grace and to Jesse, and now she'd have to apologize to Mitch too. It seemed she'd only stirred up trouble with the people she cared for. Maybe it would be better for everyone if she just left town.

But if she returned to Manhattan, who would be there for her?

Chapter 35

SUZANNE

Suzanne held the front door of Creations on Main open, her grin as wide as the doorway. A group of senior citizens loaded with purchases filed out the door and onto their tour bus. Who said senior citizens lived on Social Security alone? Not this bunch. If she didn't sell even one more item, the day would still be a highly profitable one.

She waved goodbye to the ladies and closed the door. When she retired, would she have expendable income like they did? Until a few days ago, she always thought she would. Now, only the Lord knew.

From the corner of her eye, she noticed Marla's BMW zooming into a nearby parking spot. She waved as Marla dashed toward her, all dolled up in designer clothes. Suzanne, in jeans and a sweatshirt, chuckled as she opened the door again.

"Got a minute?" Marla said, a little breathless.

"Come on in. Rob's in the back room, but we can talk at my desk." She boosted her petite body on top of it and motioned for Marla to take the chair.

Marla's eyes went immediately to the newspaper smack in the middle of the desk.

"I guess I have an idea of what's on your mind." Suzanne said.

Marla pressed a hand across her face.

Rob came out from the back room. "Oh ... hi, Marla." He looked at Suzanne, now signaling him with her facial expression. He backed up. "Well, I guess you'll be tied up for a while."

"Good guess, sweetie." Suzanne gave him a wink. "We're having some girl talk."

"Got it." He disappeared.

Suzanne hoped no customers would interrupt them, either. As much as she needed sales, right now, Marla needed her more.

"You've read it?" Marla flicked the paper with a fingertip.

"I have."

"I don't know where to begin." But apparently Marla did know where to begin, because she didn't hesitate to unload her troubles. The newspaper article. Grace so upset. Mitch unfairly accused. Rachel's irrational fears. Penny's lies.

Hard as it was, Suzanne kept quiet through it all. There were times she wanted to jump in, but she managed to keep quiet. Even without Rob reminding her, she knew that people usually needed an ear more than words of advice.

"So," Marla finally said, "the bottom line is this—I'm going to go back to New York. I don't belong here. Even Mitch says I stand out like a swan in a coal mine."

Suzanne could keep quiet no longer. "I think Mitch probably meant that as a compliment."

"Maybe, but I think there's truth to what he said. I don't fit in with the people of Port Mariette. I've been here not even one stinking week and look at the mess I've created."

She stood up, a resolute look on her face. "Yes, I'm going back home."

Suzanne dropped her jaw. "I'm shocked. I never knew you to be someone who ran away from her troubles."

"I'm not running away," Marla huffed. "I'm just giving people what they want. No changes. No interference from some rich New Yorker."

"And what will you tell Grace? That you don't have the courage to stand up for what's right? That you let someone like Penny or Rachel stand in your way? I don't believe it."

"It's more than that. I've got to try to make things right with Warren too. Out of sight, out of mind. If I don't go back now, there's no chance we'll ever get back together."

"You're sure you want to do that?"

"Yes."

Suzanne didn't believe her. Yet, she didn't try to change Marla's mind. She had been through enough relationship troubles of her own to know Marla and Warren were history, but it was not her place to tell her friend.

Marla would have to figure that out on her own.

Chapter 36

RACHEL

"You available to talk now?" Rachel put her phone close to her ear.

"Yes," Penny whispered on the other end. "But I can only talk a few minutes."

"That's fine. I'm busy too. Someone just called in a huge order." Rachel almost said *Dom called in a huge order* but caught herself in time. He'd be furious if Port Mariette's biggest gossip learned Rachel prepared meals for his restaurant.

"Busy hands are happy hands." Penny cackled, probably delighting in the uproar going on. Nothing like a spotlight on the mayor to make her happy.

"Marla was here this morning, and the conversation didn't go well," Rachel said. "You know how she is. Once she lands on an idea, there's no stopping her. We've got to come up with a way to block her before she gets carried away."

"And whatever we do," Penny said, "we've got to do it fast—before she learns we have practically no zoning restrictions in Port Mariette."

"No zoning restrictions?" Rachel sucked in a breath. "I never knew that."

Penny sniffed, as if offended. "Plenty of small towns like ours don't bother with all those rules and regulations."

"Are you saying if she asks the township for a variance on her spa, we couldn't deny It? That she could turn it into any kind of housing she wants because there's no regulation to begin with—is that what you're saying?" Rachel voice got louder as she spoke.

"That's what I'm saying. I already talked with my contact at the Pennsylvania Department of Environmental Protection. He couldn't come up with a reason to deny Marla's plan either."

"The DEP?" Rachel couldn't imagine the connection. "What on earth does Marla's housing plan have to do with the environment?"

"I'll admit it was a longshot, but I've got a good contact there, and if the DEP foresaw any kind of environmental impact issue, they could drown Marla in bureaucratic obstacles. They do have a lot of ridiculous rules, you know."

"Red tape—a great idea. Too bad it won't work." Rachel had to hand it to Penny. She might have a reputation for being crafty, even sleazy and unethical, but she took her role as mayor seriously. Turned over every stone.

"So," Penny said, kind of breathlessly, "when I saw I wouldn't get anywhere with the environmental angle, I asked Fred to come up with some new regulations for housing. If we hustle, I think we can get some kind of zoning ordinance in place before Marla takes any formal action."

"So, you're on top of it." Relief washed across Rachel's face.

"Well, we're not quite there yet. The zoning committee—that's me and Fred—will meet the day after tomorrow. Walt

'Tis the Time,' 'Tis the Season

put a teeny-tiny notice in the newspaper, so we can say it was a public meeting."

"I never saw it." Rachel tittered.

"It'll be in tomorrow's paper. So what you need to do is round up your PMBA directors. Maybe some key members too—the ones you can trust. Tell them our plan and ask them to show up for the zoning meeting. Of course, you'll want to coach them on what to say. I've already prepped my council members.

"Brilliant. And then afterwards Walt will be able to report that a cross-section of the town showed their support for the new zoning regulations."

"Exactly. I think it'll work, don't you?" Penny asked.

"Sounds like a sure-fire plan," Rachel said, "as long as Marla doesn't find out about it."

Chapter 37

MARLA

Even after nine hours of sleep, Marla woke up tired. Yesterday had been a long day, and today, she had to face both Grace and Mitch. Grace deserved an explanation, and Mitch, a big apology.

She padded downstairs in her nightgown. Coffee. That had to come first.

In the kitchen, Grace was already dressed, adjusting the dial at the toaster oven.

"You're getting your own breakfast?" Marla had become accustomed to carting it upstairs for her.

"I feel good today. Besides, I've got to get back into the swing of things soon." She turned and leaned against the counter, her elbows bent above it. "Any idea how much longer you'll be staying in town?"

Did Grace want her to leave? Or was she reading Marla's mind?

"If you're ready to handle things on your own, I can leave now. I don't want to cause any more trouble between us." Marla's shoulders drooped and her eyes beseeched her daughter's understanding.

"I talked about that newspaper article with Jesse." Grace stared at her toes. "He just laughed it off. He said, this is Port Mariette—what do you expect?" She looked up. "You know what? He's right. Stories here get blown out of proportion all the time just because there's so little going on."

The toaster oven dinged but Grace ignored it. "I guess I owe you an apology. I'm sorry. I know you are just trying to be supportive of me. Can you forgive me for being upset with you?"

Marla had to put a hand on the wall to steady herself. What a surprising start to the morning. "Of course I forgive you. And I do understand why you were upset. I got carried away, like I tend to do. I should have talked with you first. So, can you forgive me too?" She stepped toward Grace, her arms outstretched.

They had a good hug. Then they laughed.

Suddenly, Marla's world shifted. Every problem seemed less significant than it had only a few minutes ago.

"How about a bagel?" Grace brought the bagel and cream cheese to the table. "Have a seat. It's my turn to wait on you."

Marla didn't protest. She plopped onto a chair and took a bite.

Grace toasted another bagel and joined her a minute later. "Once I cooled down, I realized your idea was not only incredibly thoughtful but also wildly generous. We'd be repurposing a huge mansion—such an expensive undertaking—for a lasting and meaningful reason. I know you've got the finances to do it, but I also know you could spend your money in a million other ways. Are you sure you are committed to this?"

"If it's what you want to do," Marla said, "I'm with you one-hundred percent."

Grace's face lit up. "It is exactly what I want to do."

"Well, then," Marla said, "let's figure out the next step."

'Tis the Time,' 'Tis the Season

Chapter 38

SUZANNE

As they headed to Dom's, Suzanne glanced at Rob, sitting behind the wheel of her mother's car. Every part of his body fascinated her, even though right now, she couldn't see much but one side of his face and a hand. Skin still tan. That won't last much longer in this town.

"Maybe we should eat at home instead of splurging at Dom's," Suzanne said.

"We can still afford to dine out." Rob patted her thigh. "At least, once or twice a year."

"Very funny. You know I'm still worried. We don't have much of an action plan for paying that bill."

"We've prayed, and we're doing everything we can right now," Rob said. "I have every confidence the Lord will guide us through this."

Suzanne tipped her head. "That's exactly what I said to Penny last year when she was in the middle of her bankruptcy mess. We prayed, and then, we sat waiting until we got an answer. Herbie ended up buying her golf course, and Mitch bought her country club."

"There's a solution for us too." He smiled. "Maybe your paintings will become world famous and sell for millions."

"Maybe your books will do the same." She reached to rub the back of his neck. He wasn't tense at all. She had to let go of all this worrying. Didn't the nuns always say worrying was a sin?

"Let's take a detour along Millionaire's Row," Suzanne said, pointing to a sign reading *Hilltop Lane*. Anything for a pleasant distraction. "That street always has the most beautiful Christmas decorations in all of Port Mariette."

"I remember those lights from last winter," Rob said as he turned onto the street. "You brought me here when you took me on my first tour of the town."

"Doesn't it look magical?" Suzanne commented on each house as they inched along. "That's Dr. Hess's house with all the tall decorated evergreens, and next to it is Lipton Funeral Home with the nativity display. Look over there at Mitch's house." She jutted her chin. "The one with the *porte-cochere* on the side. Do you remember?"

"There you go with that French again." His eyes twinkled.

"Oh, you know what that means." Suzanne gave him a gentle slap on the arm. "The covered entrance on the side of the house."

"It's a nice touch of nostalgia. He's got beautiful landscaping, and his house is a stunner. In fact, this whole street is filled with magnificent homes, every one of them well maintained."

Suzanne pointed to her right. "That's Mary Frances's house, the Queen Anne. What a jewel that place is. I've never been inside it, but everyone always said it has the best view of the river."

Rob stopped the car in front of it. "Wow, what a beaut."

"There's no realtor's sign on the lawn. Maybe she's already sold it." Suzanne lightly snorted. "Probably to someone in Rachel's family."

Rob ignored her comment. "I wonder what the asking price was."

"Probably as much as my one-bedroom condo up in Pittsburgh would sell for." Suzanne hoped she could hold onto it. Located midway between Jill's house north of Pittsburgh and Port Mariette a half-hour south, with an unbeatable view of the Point in downtown Pittsburgh, it was the best investment she'd ever made. She dreaded the thought of losing it, but they might need the money.

Reaching the end of Millionaire's Row, they drove a few more blocks and arrived at Dom's.

"It looks exactly like when we were here last Christmas," Rob said, as he pulled into a parking spot and pointed to the blow up Santa. "Very romantic."

Suzanne rolled her eyes and laughed. The place actually did seem romantic, at least to her.

Inside, a tattooed hostess greeted them and ushered them under the arch decked out with fake mistletoe—the same spot where Rob had proposed to her last year.

As they passed beneath the mistletoe, Suzanne couldn't resist. She threw her arms around Rob's neck, stretched up on tiptoes, and gave him a big kiss. "I hit the jackpot when I married you, babe," she whispered in his ear. As hard as life was for them right now, she knew they'd climb this hill together. She held onto him a few seconds longer, not wanting to let go of him or the moment.

The hostess stood waiting at their table holding two large plastic-coated menus in one hand, with the other hand resting on the back of a chair. Chuckling, she said to them, "Did you two come for the meal or the mistletoe?"

"Both." Suzanne and Rob said, looking at one another and laughing.

They took their seats, and Suzanne ordered the pasta primavera, a meal she was sure came from Rachel's commercial kitchen. What the heck. Even if they were no longer friends, Rachel's cooking would always be better than anything Dom's kitchen staff prepared.

Relaxing over a glass of Riesling, Rob leaned back in his chair. "I have to say, Dom's a smart guy. He makes a lot of money from work someone else does without incurring all the costs."

"What do you mean?" Suzanne was always interested in learning ways to make money, and now, even more so.

"Dom gets great meals from Rachel, and that keeps his staffing costs down. All his cooks do with almost everything on the menu is heat and serve, then they slide it onto a clean plate. Of course, Rachel benefits too. I'll bet she does a tremendous volume with a busy place like this."

"Uh-huh," Suzanne said, her mind drifting.

"Speaking of Rachel, I hope you two can smooth things over. You have a lot of history. It'd be a shame to lose such a longtime friend."

"Rob—" Suzanne ignored his comment and pointed to a gaudy abstract painting of a cluster of grapes. "Look at that picture over there."

Rob shrugged. "Not my taste."

"Not mine, either. It's hideous, in fact. I don't know anyone—other than obviously Dom—who would like that print."

"Offends your artistic sensibility?"

Suzanne didn't respond. Her eyes darted around the room for a moment, then she grabbed Rob's arm. "You know what Dom should put on that wall? Paintings on consignment—from Creations on Main. Just like he makes money from putting Rachel's food on his tables, he could make money from hanging my paintings on his walls."

She gripped the edge of the table in excitement. "In fact, all the businesses along Main Street could make money—the bank, the insurance agency, the dentist's office, the hospital, the professional offices—every place people visit."

Rob's eyes lit up. "Terrific idea."

And if this idea works, Creations on Main won't have a backlog of inventory—meaning, no need for extra retail space or hiring more staff at another location."

"You won't need those extra shelves, either." Rob playfully jabbed Suzanne. "All of which will leave us with extra time to fill." He ran his finger along her arm.

"Hmm." Suzanne's eyes twinkled. "I wonder what we'll do with all that time?"

Chapter 39

RACHEL

Rachel was first to arrive at the country club's executive suite, but she wasn't alone for long. Soon afterwards, a couple dozen PMBA members filed into the room, their faces serious. Today, there'd be no joking around.

She began the meeting as soon as everyone had taken their seats, even though it was a few minutes short of seven a.m.

"Don't bother taking minutes this morning, Herbie," she said, not wanting any formal record of their discussion. "I just want to update you everyone about the spa situation. I'm assuming you've all read about it in the paper."

"Of course we have," Dr. Hess said a little testily. "But here's the question—are the rumors true?" He eyed both Rachel and Walt.

"I'm not able to reveal my sources," Walt said, "but I have every reason to believe it's true. Otherwise, I wouldn't have printed it."

"I tried to talk to Marla about it." Rachel spoke slowly, wanting to choose her words well. "But she made it clear she wasn't going to share her plans with me. I don't know if she's planning to have foster families in that house or if it will be young adults who have aged out of the foster care system. Either way, I don't think any of us want a lot of them living here in Port Mariette. Does everyone agree?"

Herbie spoke up first. "Actually, a bunch of those kids have been coming by my pizza shop lately. Sometimes they're a little loud, but to be honest, they're good customers. They order extra-large pizzas with lots of toppings, and soft drinks. Most people get the medium and ask for free water. With ice. And lemon. Nope, you won't find me complaining about them at all."

"Well," Dr. Hess said in his scratchy voice, "seems to me, young people need dental care, and if there are foster parents, they would too. Fillings and cleanings, that's my bread and butter." He leaned back in his chair, knocking his cane off the back. "But can these young people pay their bills?" He shrugged. "That I don't know for sure, but I have my doubts."

Next to him, Joe the barber picked the cane up from the floor and hooked it on Dr. Hess's chair. "They'd need haircuts too," Joe said, "but if any of them are Black, I don't know how to cut that kind of hair, and I don't want to be sued for discrimination. You know how it is these days, people sue you for every little perceived injustice."

The rest of the board members voiced assorted reasons for preventing the spa to be converted into anything different. After everyone had their say, Rachel leaned forward. "Confidentially," she said in a hushed tone, "I've learned from Penny that Port Mariette has absolutely no zoning regulations that would prevent Marla from turning the spa into housing for older foster kids or foster families."

"Well, that's just great," Dr. Hess said sarcastically. "What are we going to do now?"

'Tis the Time, 'Tis the Season

"Penny and I came up with a plan." Rachel smiled smugly. "There will be a zoning committee meeting at six this evening. Walt has posted a notice about it in the paper." She held up her copy of the paper. Everyone squinted in an attempt to read it.

"I have copies," Walt said, passing them out.

"Thanks, Walt." Rachel continued. "At tonight's meeting, Penny and Fred will announce some small but significant changes to the zoning regulations. These changes will prohibit any kind of group home setting or having more than five unrelated people living in the same house, even if it's converted into apartments. That should cover the bases."

She lifted her chin in Walt's direction. "Then, since Walt will attend the meeting, he'll be able to report that no one raised any objections to the zoning changes."

"That's fast work, Rachel," said Dr. Hess. "Maybe you'll turn out to be a good PMBA president after all."

Chris Posti

'Tis the Time,' 'Tis the Season

Chapter 40

MARLA

With today being one of those rare December days when the temperature was predicted to reach the high sixties, Marla felt giddy with early spring fever. In strappy sandals and a flowing skirt she'd borrowed from Grace, she headed out the door carrying a straw picnic basket and a blanket. All she needed to complete the springtime look was a daisy in her hair.

She headed toward her favorite spot in all of the spa's fifty acres—a clearing surrounded by a thicket of white pines. On a patch of sunny ground, she unfurled a blanket and placed the picnic basket in the center.

While arranging the food, she spotted Mitch loping toward her in fresh blue jeans and a T-shirt. She got herself comfortable on the blanket, crossing her legs yoga-style, and waited for him.

Already chuckling, Mitch stopped a few feet before her and took in the setting. Hands on his hips, he slowly shook his head. "Oh, boy, I think I'm going to get an apology today."

Marla tossed back her hair in mock irritation. "Don't steal my thunder." She smiled at him. "Where would you like to receive your apology—on the blanket or over there, on the bench?"

"Your pick. Just so I get it, that's all that matters."

Marla chose the bench. It would be easier if she didn't have to look him in the eye. She got up from the blanket and took a seat on one side of the bench.

Mitch stood in front of it, eyeing her as she smoothed her skirt.

"I like the skirt. Very pretty. Especially on a pretty lady."

"Thank you." Marla patted the seat so Mitch would sit down. Sweet compliment, but she wanted to get this over with.

He folded himself onto the bench and crossed an ankle over his knee.

Shoulder to shoulder, their bodies touched.

"Hm," Mitch said. "This reminds me of when we sat together eating hoagies at the Fourth of July festival. Remember that?"

Of course Marla remembered. They both smelled like pine trees after having toiled together with a dozen others to clear the highway entrance into town before the arts festival began. Her fingernails still had dirt underneath them when they downed their lunch that day. Warren showed up near the end of the meal, and when she told him she'd be staying longer in Port Mariette to be with Grace, he left in a huff.

The beginning of their end? She hadn't seen it then, but she did now.

She also remembered the feeling she had sitting next to Mitch that day, an inexplicable attraction between two people from vastly different worlds, yet still a deep connection.

And now, she felt it again. A feeling she was sitting next to a real man, not a suit. That she didn't have to be anyone but herself. She could lose the trappings of wealth, the veneer of Manhattan, and just be the woman she was inside. It felt so freeing.

"Remember that day?" he repeated, bringing Marla back to earth.

"Yes, I remember." Marla spoke softly. Did her voice betray her thoughts?

"Warren was with you that day." Mitch said it gently, as if he didn't want to dredge up the memory. "I thought after that you might never see him again."

"What made you think that? He didn't say anything in front of you, did he?"

"I saw him storm out of the festival." Mitch shook his head. "Yep, I thought you two were history."

"How ironic you'd say that. Warren and I are done."

"Really?" Mitch turned his head toward Marla. "You won't be seeing Warren anymore?"

"No. It's over."

Mitch scrunched his lips. "Sorry. I'm sure it's painful for you."

"Thanks. It's probably for the best."

"I agree. Never cared for the guy."

Surprised, she twisted her head toward him. "Why not?"

"Nothing wrong with being the smartest person in the room. But acting like you are doesn't go over well with me."

Now that she thought about it, Mitch was right. Why had she never noticed that arrogance about Warren? Was it because she behaved the same way? Or was she so taken with his power and position that she'd failed to notice?

"Sometimes I wonder if I come across that way—do I?" Marla hoped Mitch's answer would be kind.

"Only sometimes. But I don't mind. Usually you have a good reason for it." His mouth twitched into a smile. "So, then, are you planning to stay a while in Port Mariette?

Renovating the spa will require a lot of your attention, you know."

Marla shook her head. "Grace is recovering fast. I'll be leaving soon."

"Really? Let me see if I have this straight. Grace needs you here in Port Mariette, and you want to help her fulfill her dream, but you are going back to Manhattan, even though you and Warren are finished. Did I get it right?"

Marla rolled her eyes. "All Grace needs from me now is some money. I can send it to her from New York."

"You think that'll take care of everything?"

"I do more harm than good when I'm here. Look at how I stepped all over Grace's dream. I took charge of something that wasn't mine to take charge of. Along the way, I got the whole town in an uproar. I insulted you, accused you of something I should have known you would never do." She hung her head. "I am so sorry, Mitch. Can you forgive me?"

He reached an arm around her shoulders and gave her a light hug, "Of course I do."

She reached up and squeezed his fingertips. "Thank you."

They sat in that position for a while, Mitch's arm around Marla, and Marla holding onto his hand. A sudden wind blew a long strand of hair across Marla's face.

Mitch brushed it away. "Perfect day, isn't it?"

"Yes. Perfect." Marla rested her head on Mitch's shoulder. Doing so felt natural, and she drank in the feeling. Maybe it was her relief over apologizing. Or Mitch's kind reaction to it. Or could it be something else?

They sat in silence for quite a while, absorbing the sun on their skin, breathing in the warm air, taking in the moment.

Marla continued to mull the shift in her thinking. What had she ever seen in Warren? Why had she never seen all the things she now saw in Mitch?

She straightened her spine. "I've got a crick in my neck." She twisted her neck from side to side. "I think it's from sitting at the computer so much the past few days."

Mitch put his strong hand on her neck and massaged it gently. "Does this help?"

She could feel the emotion in his fingers. It was flowing right into her. This was insane, having this new kind of feeling for Mitch. He was a good friend, a trusted advisor, her contractor. Nothing more.

But there *was* more, she had to admit. She could not deny a physical attraction, a strong one. Mitch's weathered face, his smiling eyes, his sinewy arms, his resonant voice, his earthy, outdoorsy scent. He smelled like a man ought to, not like a bottle of manufactured cologne.

On the inside, he had unexpected qualities too. Different ones. Appealing ones. He'd shown himself to be a man of faith, of character, of integrity. In so many ways, Mitch was the opposite of Warren. The realization boggled her mind.

"Are you going to the zoning meeting tonight?" Mitch said, jarring her from her thoughts.

It took her a moment to respond. "What are you talking about?"

"I got a call from Herbie this morning. Seems our conniving mayor has scheduled a public meeting to approve some zoning changes."

"I never heard a thing about it." Marla looked him in the eye.

"Unless you saw the fine print in the *Port Mariette Gazette*, you would have missed it. Check out the bottom of the last page. The meeting's tonight at six."

"Wow." She patted her lips as she considered the news. "This has got to be about the spa."

"Undoubtedly. Will you be there? Or will you be busy packing?"

Chapter 41

SUZANNE

Suzanne peeked into the front window of Hair & Care, where Sharon was blow-drying an older woman's short gray hair. Considering all the wind today, the customer could have just as easily come outside to let it dry naturally.

While waiting, Suzanne mouthed the words of her pitch. As a former trainer, she was accustomed to speaking confidently and persuasively, but in her training days, she followed a script. Off-the-cuff didn't come to her so easily, and she knew practicing out loud would prove much more effective than merely thinking about what she'd say.

She paced back and forth rehearsing until the newly coiffed customer exited, then she slid inside.

Sitting at the front desk, Sharon glanced up, surprised to see her. "Back again? Are you making an appointment? Or are you still hoping to get some of these handmade Christmas decorations for your shop?" Her smile was not genuine.

"Actually, I did want to make an appointment."

The look of surprise returned to Sharon's face. "Really?"

"Yes. I had an appointment scheduled back home, but obviously I had to cancel it." Suzanne tipped her head forward. "My roots need a touch-up."

"They sure do." Sharon clicked a few keys on her keyboard. "How about the day after tomorrow at ten?" She looked up over her glasses at Suzanne.

"Works for me." Suzanne turned, pretending she was leaving, then reversed herself. "By the way, what will you be putting on your walls when you take down the Christmas decorations?"

"Nothing much. Just some photos of women in different hairstyles." Sharon cackled. "Kinda out of date ones, if you really want to know."

"I was wondering ... would you like to make some money from those walls?"

Sharon arched a dark manicured brow. "How?"

"I could hang some paintings from Creations on Main—acrylics, oils, drawings, anything you want." Suzanne leaned over the desk to whisper. "Whatever you sell, you'd get to keep ten percent."

Sharon took a look at the wall next to her, then back at Suzanne, then back to another wall, as if sizing up how much space she'd have and how much money she could make.

"If you can do twenty percent," she said in a low voice, "you have a deal."

Twenty percent. That's twice what Suzanne had decided on. If she gave Sharon twenty percent, she'd have to give that to everyone else. They'd all find out within days. She should have gone to the coffee shop first. They probably wouldn't have tried to negotiate like Sharon. But over there, Suzanne didn't know the owner. She'd assumed by scheduling a hair appointment, she could get Sharon on board with her idea.

'Tis the Time,' 'Tis the Season

Suzanne pursed her lips. *No.* Twenty percent was too much. She just couldn't agree to it. Deflated, she let out a sigh. "Sorry. I can't do twenty."

Sharon didn't say anything.

Suzanne knew better than to fill that vacuum. She adjusted the shoulder strap on her purse. She'd try the coffee shop next. "Well, see you soon."

"Y'know what?" Sharon crossed her arms. "I don't make a penny off these Christmas decorations. When I take them down, I'd like to put up something nice and new—and I'd like even more to make ten percent off whatever my customers buy."

"Ten percent—great!" Suzanne reached over the desk and gave Sharon a strong handshake. "It's a deal."

Marla was right. Back when Suzanne lost her job as an airline trainer Marla had told Suzanne she'd make a good salesperson. She'd have to tell Marla how she negotiated her deal with Hair & Care. Maybe she'd also ask Marla if she could ask Warren for a boilerplate agreement for consignment sales. Suzanne certainly didn't want to spend a dime paying for one.

Chapter 42

RACHEL

Moving as fast as a short-order cook, Rachel microwaved two bowls of chicken soup and threw together some sandwiches. As soon as Pete came in the door, she hollered, "Dinner's on the table."

"Already?" Pete scratched his head as he strode into the kitchen. "It's not even three o'clock."

"Big meeting tonight."

Rachel sat down and pulled a couple paper napkins from the dispenser on the kitchen table. Without waiting for Pete, she crossed herself, said a quick prayer, and picked up her chipped ham sandwich.

"What time's the meeting?" He slid into a chair and took his first spoonful.

"Six. But I have to do a few things first. I wanna beat that storm too. It's blowing in fast."

Rachel hated to drive in bad weather. She'd asked Tony to come with her so he could drive, but he claimed he had a cold and didn't want to spread his germs. White lie or not, she knew the truth. He wouldn't want to get caught in the middle between her and his good buddy Herbie, who seemed to like the young people from August Village—or at least the sales they registered at his pizza place.

Even if Tony didn't come, though, she wouldn't be the only concerned citizen. Plenty of other folks would fill up the township's meeting room. If the weather got really nasty, she could always bum a ride home with someone else.

Pete swallowed another spoonful. "Early dinner's always fine by me." No wonder. He opened Food 'n Fuel at seven every morning.

"Soup's great, Mom. Love that old world taste. You can't get that out of a can."

How nice of Pete to notice. "I always make it exactly the way Grandma used to make it. Everything's fresh, right down to the bay leaf."

Pete slurped another spoonful, just like Stan used to. Those two were so alike. Sometimes she got this strange feeling, just for a flash, where it seemed like Pete was Stan, alive again and young. But the image would leave in an instant, and she'd miss Stan all over again.

Maybe she didn't miss his slurping, but Stan wouldn't have faked a cold to get out of an awkward situation like Tony did. Still, Tony had plenty of good qualities. He paid attention to her. Said nice things to her. Noticed her hair. Knew how to touch her. He was fun and made her feel young again. So what if he didn't come to the meeting tonight? She didn't need a man to lean on. Not anymore. She could drive in any kind of weather or at night, even if she didn't like to, or get a ride with someone else.

He'd better show up for her Christmas dinner, though. No excuses for missing that.

Pete took a big bite of his sandwich. "What's for dessert?"

'Tis the Time,' Tis the Season

Rachel jutted her chin to a plate on the kitchen counter. "Chocolate chip cookies."

"Yum." His mouth full, he still managed to speak and smile. Just like Stan used to.

How she wished Stan were here for Christmas. With him gone and the other kids on a ski trip with their families, the table would seem so empty. How could freezing your buns off on some mountain be better than spending Christmas with your family?

"I'm so glad Lindsey will be coming over for Christmas dinner, but I wish your brothers and their families would be here too."

"Yeah, what does Vail have over Port Mariette?" Pete chortled, but Rachel pretended she didn't hear him.

"I'll really miss seeing the grandkids." She wagged her finger at Pete. "Mark my words, one of these days when you have gray hair, you'll know what I mean. There's nothing like grandkids. They light up your life like nobody else."

Pete finished his sandwich and wiped the edges of his mouth with his thumb. "Well, next Christmas, you'll have another grandkid, right here in Port Mariette."

"I can't wait." Rachel grinned. Thank goodness she had one son who would raise his family here.

She looked at the clock. Plenty of time to wash her hair, maybe even paint her nails for a change. "Well, I guess I'll go upstairs and get cleaned up. How about putting the dishes in the dishwasher for me? And could you feed Cinders too?" She pushed her chair back and rose from it.

"Sure, but before you go, do you have a minute?"

Rachel let herself back down. By the look in his eyes, she knew this would be big.

Chapter 43

MARLA

Dark clouds moving in dropped the temperature fast, forcing an end to Marla's picnic with Mitch. They quickly returned to the spa, and once Mitch drove off, Marla rushed up the front steps, her hair and skirt blowing about in the wind.

Mitch's touch as well as his words were fighting for her attention, but she wouldn't allow those thoughts to control her mind right now. Grace's dream was on the line. So little time to prepare, yet Marla had to be ready.

She stepped inside the spa.

Grace glanced up from her computer screen. "Oh, you're finally back. I was getting ready to call the missing persons bureau." She smiled. "How'd the picnic go?"

"Wonderful." Marla dropped the basket and blanket on the chair next to Grace's desk. "But Mitch told me something upsetting—Penny has planned some kind of zoning meeting tonight in the administration building. You and I have got to be there." She looked over Grace's shoulder at the screen. "Do we have any clients booked this evening?"

"What do you mean, a zoning meeting?" Grace rolled back in her chair to let Marla see the appointments.

Marla repeated everything Mitch had told her. "Who knows what Penny has planned? We've got to show up." She tilted her head toward the screen. "There are only a few appointments booked tonight. Can't Hannah or Latoya handle things on their own while we're gone?"

Grace shrugged. "You can go to the meeting if you want, but I'm staying here. I don't want to make any enemies." She looked up at Marla, still hovering over her. "Maybe you should stay home too. Just let things be. Jesse and I will figure something out that doesn't upset the whole town."

"Look, Grace. I believe I can make the case that converting the spa will be good for Port Mariette, and I think I can say it in a way that won't rile anyone up."

Grace sighed. "I can't stop you from attending, but please don't stir up animosity, especially against the foster kids. We're trying to help them, not hurt them."

"I'll behave myself. I promise." Marla put her hand over her heart and went upstairs to get ready.

★★★

A few minutes before six, Marla arrived at the meeting room. The crowd hushed as Marla made her way to a seat. Along the way, she saw plenty of faces she didn't recognize and body language that made it clear she and her ideas were not welcome. She could feel her heart pounding a little. Maybe Grace was right about staying home—but Marla couldn't turn back now.

Penny opened the meeting, pretending to be surprised by the size of the crowd. "This is just a little meeting to inform the public about a few zoning changes. I'm pleasantly surprised to see this kind of participation from our community." She tipped her head toward the row of windows. "Especially with a storm moving in."

Before Penny went any further, Marla got out of her seat, pen and paper in hand, and strode to the front of the room. She would not wait for permission to speak.

As she neared the lectern, Penny backed away toward the windows. If Mitch hadn't pulled his feet away in time, she would have tripped over them.

With Penny hovering on the side of the room, Marla turned her attention to the crowd. Row by row, her eyes took in their faces. She smiled at every person, hoping being congenial would catch them off guard. Mitch gave her a supportive wink, and she gave him a long look so he'd know she'd seen it.

"Good evening," she finally said to the crowd. Her heart still pounding, she took in a calming breath and continued. "I think we all know why we are here. Every one of us understands what's really going on, right?" She willed herself to smile again. "I don't want to be disruptive, but before anyone talks about zoning, it seemed logical for me to tell you the plans I'm making for the spa. That way, you can make an informed decision."

She cast a passing glance at Walt sitting in the front row next to Mitch. "Since I wasn't interviewed for the article in the paper, it seems there's been a lot of speculation, but not necessarily a lot of truth. Maybe that's why many of you came here this evening—to get the whole story." She liked Walt, despite his shoddy journalism, and her statement was the nicest possible way to let everyone know he hadn't interviewed her for his headline story.

She forged on. "In case you're wondering, I am planning to convert the spa into a residence for young people transitioning out of foster care, or possibly foster families who need an affordable place to live. Maybe both. Right now, I don't know which direction I'll go. My daughter, Grace, will manage daily operations. Financially, I might give some kind of grant to the tenants, according to their need. Again, I don't know all the details yet."

Hearing murmuring, she spoke a little more forcefully. "As I'm sure you know, it's my right to disburse money from my foundation however I see fit, as long as the grant aligns with its mission, which is to revitalize our local economy now that the steel and coal industries have left the valley. You probably remember my foundation gave grants to redo all the facades along Main Street and put up old-fashioned streetlights." She hoped the reminder might soften their hearts.

One person called out, "Thank you, Marla." It sounded like Herbie on the left side of the room, but she wasn't sure. If she acknowledged his comment with a thank-you, others might be encouraged to shout out, so she ignored it and continued.

"I understand some people have been focusing on potential negatives of my plan. I'm asking you to consider instead how the change will impact Port Mariette positively."

Grumbling began from the back of the room. To divert attention, she held up her index finger. "For one thing, the tax base will increase." Second finger up. She had to speak a little louder to overcome the sound of people now calling out their opinions. "Young people will be available for work." Third finger. "People who have purchasing power will spend money at our local shops and restaurants, as well as for medical, dental, insurance, and legal services."

She took another breath. "What's more—"

Sharon from Hair & Care interrupted in a deep, loud voice. "You can spin it any way you want, Marla, but I've

'Tis the Time, 'Tis the Season

said it before, and I'll say it again—this is *not going to happen in my back yard*. N-I-M-B-Y!"

Immediately, a few others spoke, talking over one another. Whether for or against the concept, in their zeal to make their position known, no one could be heard.

Marla attempted to rationally address questions and concerns, but the noise would not allow her to be heard.

It seemed a good number of people were arguing in her favor, but then someone in the back started chanting, *NIMBY, NIMBY, NIMBY*, and others soon joined in.

Never had Marla faced such an unreasonable group. She tried to speak, but for some reason, her words came out slurred. By the looks on the faces in the audience, she knew no one could understand her.

The pen and paper fell from her left hand. With the other, she gripped onto a table.

Mitch appeared behind her and propped her up. "Can anyone help here?" Mitch called out to the room. "Carol Ann?"

Marla had no idea who Carol Ann was, but in seconds, a woman surfaced, as well as a young paramedic.

"Pull your ambulance up to the door," Carol Ann ordered him.

Mitch guided Marla to a chair and gently let her down. "Lucky you," he whispered in her ear, "you're getting the fastest medical care in the world."

With crooked lips, Marla attempted a smile.

She failed.

Chapter 44

SUZANNE

Main Street was like a ghost town tonight. A little freaky, like this evening's weather. Who could have imagined the temperature would drop so fast? Still, Suzanne was glad she and her sister could work without interruption.

Earlier in the day, Suzanne had canvassed the businesses on Main Street and made arrangements with more than a dozen of them to display paintings on consignment—all of them at a ten percent commission. When she had more time, she'd approach all the professional offices scattered around town too. And Dom's. Certainly couldn't forget Dom's.

Getting these verbal agreements was merely the first step. Next, she'd have to get something in writing.

Suzanne parked herself on the side of the desk where Andrea was marking a list with highlighters.

"I hope Warren comes through with some kind of sales agreement for us," Suzanne said. "He's such a whiz at legal stuff."

"Marla hasn't gotten back to you yet?" Andrea looked up from the spreadsheet.

"Not yet. I left her a long message, but I haven't heard from her." It wasn't like Marla to ignore a call. "Maybe she accidentally left her phone turned off." Goodness knows, Suzanne herself had done that from time to time. "Or maybe she's waiting to talk with Warren before she calls me back."

Andrea held the spreadsheet up. "Look, here's how I divvied up the inventory among all the businesses. I've color-coded about a hundred items so far. Take a gander."

Suzanne looked it over. "Who gets the items highlighted in blue? Those are some of our nicest local landscapes."

"Those will be for Hair & Care. The way I look at it, Sharon's got a captive audience staring at all those walls, and women who pay to get their hair done have money to spare. We ought to make sure her walls are full of paintings depicting Port Mariette."

"Good thinking." Andrea was doing a bang-up job orchestrating their inventory. Had Suzanne underestimated her? Or maybe Andrea was motivated by seeing how much money they could potentially make. If this took off as Suzanne expected, they'd earn some serious income. All day, Suzanne had tried not to count her chickens before they hatched, but it was exhilarating to imagine how sales from all over town would impact her finances. With any luck, she'd be able to make a big dent in that contractor bill.

Suddenly an ambulance whizzed by the shop, lights flashing and siren wailing.

Andrea headed toward the front window. "That's something you don't often see out there."

"An ambulance?" She followed Andrea. "Why not?" After all, Port Mariette was populated from one end to the other with senior citizens.

'Tis the Time,' Tis the Season

"The normal route is from Sunset Hills to Hope Hospital. That's nowhere near Main Street."

They reached the front window just in time to watch the ambulance turning, its wheels screeching as it disappeared at the far end of Main Street.

"He's driving like a maniac. Might be black ice out there." Andrea pursed her lips. "Must be something serious." She turned away from the window and went back to her spreadsheet.

Suzanne said a silent prayer, just like the nuns had taught her to do all those years ago. Some things you never forget.

Chapter 45

RACHEL

After Marla left in the ambulance, the mood in the room shifted. Zoning matters no longer seemed so important.

Whispers reigned throughout the room. Rachel stared at Penny, sunk low in a chair, staring. Would they be needing another ambulance?

Someone had to say something, and Penny seemed unable, so Rachel got up. "I think we can all agree this is not the time to discuss township zoning. Let's all go home, cool our heels, say a prayer for Marla."

Penny roused herself enough to say, "I agree." She moved to the lectern and rapped the gavel. "Meeting adjourned." She stuffed some papers into her large handbag then hurried to Herbie's side.

As the crowd shuffled out, Rachel returned to her chair and bowed her head to say a silent prayer for Marla's recovery. She walked out of the meeting alone. Schmoozing with PMBA members didn't seem to matter right now.

On her way to her car, she called Tony. "Mind if I come over?"

"You won't mind my germs?" For a guy who supposedly had a cold, Tony sounded a little too chipper.

"I'll sit on the other end of the couch," Rachel said flatly. "I need to talk."

Soon she was at his house, where he stood at the front window waiting. She kept her head down as the wind battered her face. Thankfully, she'd worn a parka with a lined hood.

He opened the door and let her in. His nose wasn't even pink, and there wasn't a tissue in sight, but he had managed to get a bottle of wine ready for them.

Still in her coat, she blurted out the details about Marla.

"Wow. I hope she's okay." He gave Rachel a soft hug.

"Me too." Rachel choked up. "I wouldn't want to lose her. Even though we disagree about the zoning issue, she's still one of my few good friends."

"You have plenty of friends." He helped her with her coat.

"Name them." She plopped onto the cushion and adjusted a throw pillow.

"Well, there's your cousin Bernadette."

"She's about a dozen years older than I am, and other than being widowed, we have nothing in common."

"How about your buddy Sandy Roczinski?" He reached for the bottle of wine and filled two glasses.

"She's busy with Ted and all his health problems. We're lucky if we can get together for an occasional church bingo."

"Now don't forget, you've got *me*." Tony reached over and tickled her.

Rachel pushed his hand away. "I know that, but I need to make things right with Marla." She took a gulp of wine. "What if it's too late? What if this is a major stroke? What if she never recovers?" Her voice kept rising as she talked.

Tony patted her arm. "I think you're overreacting. You even said she was able to walk out of the room and get into the ambulance without using a gurney."

'Tis the Time,' 'Tis the Season

"Yeah, but it sure looked like another stroke. Who knows how serious it was?"

"She'll be fine."

"I hope so." Rachel took another sip. "Heck, when she gets out of the hospital, who knows what she'll want to do about the spa."

"Whatever she does, you know she'll fight for what her daughter wants. And with all her money, Marla can overcome any obstacle—especially something stupid like a rigged zoning restriction. Maybe you should just forget about trying to stop her."

"I can't," Rachel said. "It's my responsibility to do what's best for the businesses of Port Mariette. If Marla gets away with her plans for converting the spa, it will open the floodgates for all sorts of trouble."

"Like what? What are you so afraid of?"

"Remember how Penny resisted the new highway exit because it would bring strangers into town?"

"Sure, but that wasn't her real reason for fighting it. She was playing political games for her own purposes. You know that."

"Well, she did have a point, though." Rachel poured herself another glass. "In a small town like this, it's easy to keep tabs on people. If someone's acting up, word gets around fast. Parents are involved. Teachers, neighbors, business owners. Everyone has a hand in keeping Port Mariette safe. But if strangers move here—especially ones who came out of foster care—they don't have any history here. No connections. Who knows what they might do? Maybe they'll form a gang. Or deal in drugs. We don't need any of that here."

"Well, at least they won't be homeless people setting up tents. We're lucky not to have any issues like that here." He

203

reached for his wine. "Why don't you have a conversation with Marla? Get some more information from her. Discuss her plans in detail. I think the whole town has overreacted."

Rachel sighed. "Maybe I'll do that, after she gets out of the hospital. *If* she gets out of the hospital." She could lose Marla tonight and not even have the chance to apologize. She'd never get over it. A tear ran down her cheek.

"Hey, hey, hey." Tony put his arm around her. "Don't worry. She'll be all right." He gave her a squeeze. "When she gets out of there, you can invite her to Pete's wedding. It'll give you and Marla something happy to talk about."

Rachel covered her face with both hands. "I can't believe you brought that up."

"What d'ya mean?" Tony leaned in to her.

"Pete and Lindsey are cancelling their wedding plans." Rachel wailed.

"What are you talking about? Did they break off their engagement?"

"No." She choked up, pausing until she gained control of her voice. "They're getting married, but not in a church." She broke free of Tony's embrace and reached for some tissues. "They've decided to have a civil ceremony."

"You're kidding. How come?"

Rachel downed the last of her wine as she felt the shame creeping up her spine. How could such a thing happen in her family?

"Lindsey's already pregnant."

Chapter 46

MARLA

Whether this was a mini-stroke or a full-scale one, Marla knew she was losing brain cells every second. Her situation was just like Grace's when she was hemorrhaging. Speed mattered. What a break that paramedic had driven to the zoning meeting in an ambulance. Now, if only he'd get her to the hospital without crashing.

He came to a sudden stop, and a rush of people appeared to get her into the emergency room. Someone put an IV line in her arm. Next came a CT scan. Then a doctor who was checking Marla's reflexes asked her if she'd been taking her blood thinner.

She gulped. "I'm embarrassed to say, I forgot to pack it."

He raised an eyebrow. "How many days have you skipped it?"

"About a week." She grimaced.

He left the room, and someone rolled her away for an MRI. Lying on the scanning table, she still couldn't move her left arm.

Nearly an hour later, the attendant slid her out of the tank and gave her an encouraging smile. "All done."

Marla smiled back at him. "I'm feeling better already." Perhaps a lie, but her voice did sound quite normal to her, and she was able to move her mouth just fine. Maybe she'd spoken the truth after all.

The attendant wheeled her out of the MRI room. Mitch was waiting for her, his eyes full of concern. He squeezed her left hand. "Can you feel that?"

She could! She squeezed back weakly. What a crazy feeling, like she'd again absorbed something from Mitch's hand.

"Atta girl," he said, patting her shoulder. "You'll be out of this place in no time."

"But first," the attendant said, looking down at her, "they said you have to be admitted, at least for the night."

Marla groaned.

Mitch squeezed her hand again. "Let this nice fellow take you upstairs to a room. I'll go get some coffee and meet you up there in a while."

"I have to take her back to the ER first," the attendant said. "It'll be a while before she gets to a room."

Mitch squinted at her. "You're sure you don't want me to call Grace?"

Marla shook her head. "Not yet. Let's wait a while." This time it was Marla who squeezed Mitch's hand. Their eyes met for a second before he had to let go.

Soon, she was in a room, the blinds already down, with two nurses fussing over her. A neurologist, then a cardiologist, stopped in to check on her. VIP treatment? Possibly. She'd send the hospital a donation anyway.

Finally, everyone was gone. Marla closed her eyes. She tried to still her mind, but the thoughts kept running through it without permission. The mini-stroke. The zoning meeting. August Village. Grace. Mitch. Life. Death. The loop continued until she heard someone cough.

Mitch entered, holding a plastic bag. "Got you a little gift. I figure you'll be bored to tears staying here overnight." He handed it to her. "Reading material."

"That was sweet of you." No matter what was in the bag, his thoughtfulness touched her heart.

"It's just a few magazines." He put the bag on the service tray and scraped a chair across the floor. He cleared his throat. "Grace will be coming soon. Jesse's bringing her."

"You called her?" Marla lifted her head off the pillow.

He shook his head. "No. I called Jesse. I promised you I wouldn't call Grace, but I never promised anything about Jesse. Figured he'd know how to tell Grace the news better than I would."

"That's okay." Marla lifted a shoulder. "I probably should have told you to call her right away."

Mitch smiled, looking relieved.

Marla let out a long sigh. "What a turn of events. I'm supposed to be taking care of Grace, not the other way around. This is the last thing I wanted—to be an imposition to her."

Mitch leaned toward her, his face close to hers. Softly, he said, "She's your daughter, Marla. She wants to be there for you. Why don't you just let her love you?"

Chapter 47

SUZANNE

It was almost ten p.m. when Suzanne and her sister finally locked up Creations on Main. "Whew. Long day." Suzanne dropped the key in her purse, and they made their way to their cars.

"If you get your hands on that legal agreement," Andrea said, "tomorrow will be even busier. We need to get a lot of signatures before we can hang a single picture."

"I've been thinking, maybe I shouldn't bother Marla and Warren about that agreement. It doesn't need to be a complicated document. I'll draft something and run it by you in the morning."

"Sounds like a plan." Andrea waved goodbye and hopped into her car.

On the way home, Suzanne talked into her phone, listing in an email to herself what to include in the agreement—the number of paintings per location, who would hang them and how, an understanding that there would be no responsibility for holes in the wall, how long the paintings would remain in one place before they'd get changed out, and more.

Still speaking into her phone, she reached her mother's house. Dim light shone from the living room window. If her mother were inside, she'd be in bed by now.

But it was Rob, not her mother, in the house. Her wonderful husband, wide awake and eager to see her. She couldn't wait to get inside to give him a hug.

She hurried up the porch steps and opened the door.

Rob was sitting in the upholstered chair, his hands spread wide on the armrests, staring at a piece of paper on his lap.

"Hi, honey." Suzanne walked over and greeted him with a kiss on the forehead. She glanced at the paper. The contractor's final bill. She looked at the bottom number. "Oh, my. That's more than we expected." Her consignment income wouldn't make much of a dent in a bill of that size.

Rob nodded in acknowledgment, seemingly unable to talk.

Suzanne couldn't fit in the chair with him, so she dropped beside him on the floor and rested her head on his knee.

"This is all my fault, Suzanne. I never should have self-insured that house. That was so stupid of me."

She looked up at him, full of sympathy. "Don't be so hard on yourself. I'm sure there's something we can do. Maybe we can get a home equity loan, what do you think?" Suzanne had no experience with such matters but she'd heard of others getting them.

Rob snorted. "I already have one."

"You do?" He had never told her anything about having a home equity loan. *Secrets.* They could ruin a marriage.

"I took it out when I got divorced, to cover the settlement."

Suzanne could have kicked herself. Why hadn't she dug deeper into Rob's financial state before she married him? Why couldn't he have come clean on his own? He knew she was uptight about money.

'Tis the Time,' Tis the Season

She pulled herself up to her knees and looked him in the eye. "Why didn't you ever tell me about that?"

He flinched. "It didn't seem all that important. I paid the monthly payments just like every other bill. If this ground movement problem hadn't come up, we'd be fine financially." He smacked the bill with his hand. "Who could have anticipated such a huge problem? It's an outlier."

"An outlier." Suzanne repeated the word. "I get it." She tried to sound supportive, but this financial problem dug deep into her most vulnerable place.

"I don't see a way out, Suzanne. As soon as the house is fixed, we're going to have to sell it. We just can't afford this bill along with a mortgage, even with both of our incomes." He pitched the piece of paper onto the floor.

Suzanne's mouth had gone dry. She dropped her head and silently prayed for guidance.

"I know we'll get through this," Rob said, massaging his forehead, "but at the moment, I just don't know how." He got up. "I'm whipped. I'm sure you are too. Let's go to bed." He extended a hand and pulled her up from the floor.

"Wait." Suzanne put her hands on his shoulders. "I have an idea." She paused for a breath then talked fast. "Now that my mother's house is cleaned out, I've gotten used to it. Staying here is actually better than being in my Pittsburgh condo. You see, when I'm in Port Mariette, I'm close to my mother, my sister, my friends, and my business—but when I stay in the condo, the only one I'm near to is Jill."

Rob scrunched his forehead. "Not sure I'm following."

She laughed, knowing she hadn't made much sense. "I think we ought to sell my condo in Pittsburgh. I'd get half a million for it, easy. After paying the contractor bill, we'd even have money left over."

Rob let out a long whistle. "That's incredibly generous of you, Suzanne." He pulled her in for a hug. "But you can't shoulder the responsibility for my mistakes. I want you to keep your condo. After all, you'll be visiting Jill more often once she has a second baby."

"Well, consider it as a possibility." What a relief. She didn't want to admit she'd been counting on her condo as a major part of her retirement plan.

"I think I have a better idea," Rob said, confidence rising in his voice. "You know I've always worked solo, but plenty of psychologists have staffs. Sometimes they're employees and other times, contractors. The owner and the therapists usually do a sixty-forty financial split. It's a nice arrangement. The therapists make money and so does the owner of the practice. Just for bringing in the patients and taking care of all the paperwork, I'd earn forty percent."

"Forty percent? Gee, that's a good deal. Why haven't you done it already?" Rob had been leaving a lot of money on the table. It didn't make any sense.

"Eh." He shrugged. "I always earned enough money on my own, and I didn't want to be bothered by having staff. People can drive you crazy. Even a psychologist knows that." He gave her a little wink. "But now, I'm blessed with an understanding wife, and my kids live on their own. Putting up with a little aggravation from staff members is the least I can do to get us out of this financial hole."

"But how would you find therapists to work for you? Good ones, I mean."

"I know plenty of people in my field. And with everyone doing tele-therapy now, the therapists could be located anywhere." His head jerked a smidge, as if something big had just dawned on him. "In fact, I could work from anywhere myself. Anyplace I want."

'Tis the Time,' 'Tis the Season

"Anyplace?" Where was he thinking? The beach? Another country? She had no idea.

He grabbed Suzanne's arms. "Let's sell that house in California. Those taxes and utilities are ridiculous, and if we kept it, I'd have to take out an expensive insurance policy."

"I thought you loved living in California," Suzanne said, still confused.

"I did, for many years, but I think God's telling me to make a change. After all, my son's in Seattle and my daughter's in Chicago. Besides, California's not the same as it used to be."

"Where would we live? Not here, I hope." Suzanne scrunched her nose. She didn't mind her mother's house for short visits, but as her own home? Never.

"I don't know. I haven't given it a thought until right now."

Suzanne shrugged. "I guess we could live in my condo in Pittsburgh. It's got two bedrooms, and that view of the Point is phenomenal."

"That's true, we could. Nice to have an option. We could live in your condo, or even stay right here in your mom's house, at least for a while. We'll figure it out later. For now, let's just get that Carmel Highlands house on the market."

Suzanne bounced up and down, clapping like her granddaughter. She had loved living in California, but Western Pennsylvania was home.

Chapter 48

RACHEL

Rachel wobbled as she attempted to put on her parka. "Where did that arm hole go?" She giggled like a schoolgirl as she searched for it.

"It's pretty late," Tony said, as he tried to help. "Maybe you wanna stay the night? I could sleep on the couch if you want. Or you could stay in the spare bedroom. Sheets are clean."

She looked at the empty wine bottle and let out a noticeable sigh. "Thanks, but I gotta get home." She had lectured Pete more than once about not staying out all night with Lindsey. "Now's not the time to be a hypocrite."

"Okay, but be careful, will ya?" Tony stretched an arm around her, ready to give her a kiss.

"Hey, buddy, don't you have a cold?" She tipped her head toward the box of tissues, which he hadn't touched all evening. "Or maybe you're all better." Did Tony think she didn't know why he'd skipped the meeting? She gave him a quick kiss and went to her car. A bit woozy, but she could easily make it the few blocks home, especially since the roads were dry.

She took her time backing out of Tony's long driveway. It was straight, but those giant oaks on both sides put her on edge. The wind was blowing the branches, making them look like spooky monsters coming after her.

Eventually she made it from the driveway onto the street. Creeping along Hilltop Lane, she couldn't help but marvel at all the Christmas decorations. Tonight's wine probably made them look even better than usual.

A few blocks later, she reached Main Street, its lampposts lit with strands of old-fashioned multi-colored lights, and the shops decorated with garlands of holly and Christmas trees. The whole street looked like it belonged on a Christmas card.

Until she reached Herbie's pizza shop, that is. There, the fluorescent lights looked cheap and garish, and who were all those young men inside, goofing around and laughing, especially at this late hour? She slowed down. Maybe Herbie didn't care, but someone's got to keep an eye on this town.

She pulled over and watched them a while through her yawns. When the server brought out the pizza, they seemed to calm down, so she drove on.

Only one block to home. She yawned again, long and loudly, and continued to drive.

Suddenly the car hit something, hard, and instantly, her body jerked forward to meet an inflated airbag. She panicked. It felt like she couldn't breathe.

Mercifully, someone opened her car door. Swaying sideways toward him, she gasped for fresh air, wondering if she might throw up on his flashy tennis shoes.

"You all right, ma'am?" The young man's voice said with concern.

She looked up. Two men. One Black, one White. Strangers. From August Village? She sucked in a breath.

"I'm okay," Rachel whimpered.

'Tis the Time, 'Tis the Season

"You want us to call someone? A tow truck? You aren't bleeding anywhere, are you?" They looked her over with concern. "We can walk you home if you live around here. What can we do to help you?"

Too many questions. Her head hurt. "Are you from August Village?"

"How'd you know?" One of them answered, laughing.

"I guess I stick out here a little," said the other. "Don't I?" His dark eyes shone as he laughed. "We were on our way to get some pizza."

A patrol car pulled up behind them, lights flashing. Sergeant Dan got out and strode toward them, directing a flashlight in each of their faces.

When the light was off her, Rachel grabbed a breath mint from the console and popped it into her mouth.

Sergeant Dan approached the car. "You okay, Rachel?"

"I'm fine, I'm fine." Would her voice give her away?

He eyed the young men then walked to the front of the car, examining the damage. "Somebody want to tell me what happened?"

What should she say? The telephone pole jumped in front of her car? "I ... I don't really know." An honest answer because she truly didn't know how she'd managed to hit the pole.

"She swerved to avoid hitting a cat," one of the young men said, sounding credible.

Really? Maybe she had.

"Yeah, it was a black cat," said the other one. "Hard to see him." He looked at his friend and chuckled. "We thought that cat was a goner."

Sergeant Dan rubbed his chin and looked down the street.

"Maybe it was Sandy's cat," Rachel suggested. The Roczinskis lived only a few houses away.

"Or a patch of ice," said Sergeant Dan. "That wind has been playing tricks on drivers tonight."

He walked around the car, flashing his light as he re-inspected the damage. "Well, Rachel, I'll have to call a tow truck for you. Want me to drop you off at your house?"

Her eyes darted back and forth between the Sergeant and the two young men. Finally, she smiled and said, "Home's only a block away. These nice young men have already offered to walk me there." She grabbed her tote and squeezed out from behind the airbag.

"You sure?" Sergeant Dan said, a bushy brow raised.

"Yes." She said it as convincingly as she could. "I'm still a little shook up, and I feel like walking would ease my jitters."

"Okay." He didn't sound convinced but didn't argue with her. "I'll get your car towed to Artie's Body Shop, if that's all right with you."

"Sure." Her Stan had been good friends with Artie. Surely he'd fix her car for a reasonable price.

"Judging by the damage, you might end up with a new vehicle instead of fixing this one."

"Oh." Rachel twitched the side of her mouth. Lately, she'd been thinking the president of PMBA should have a new model vehicle. But now, maybe not.

"All right. Let me have your car key." Sergeant Dan took it, then wagged his finger at her with mock seriousness. "You get home now and take care of yourself."

"Will do." She gave him a salute and joined the young men waiting on the sidewalk.

"I live right down there." She pointed to a house not far off, and they headed in that direction. As soon as she heard Sergeant Dan's car door slam, she said, "I owe you guys, big time."

'Tis the Time, 'Tis the Season

Chapter 49

MARLA

"I mean it," Marla said to Grace on the other end of the line. "There's absolutely no need for you and Jesse to rush over to the hospital. Really. It was just a mini-stroke, and it was my own fault. I forgot to pack my blood pressure meds." Marla paused to listen. "Okay. Thanks for your prayers, Grace. Love you." She put the phone back on the service tray and looked at Mitch, sitting at her bedside.

"You've been praying for me too, haven't you?"

He nodded. "Of course I have."

"I need to do more of that. Praying, I mean." Marla looked to the wall then back at Mitch. "I've been doing a lot of thinking. Wondering what the future might bring, that sort of thing." She shrugged.

"Lying in a hospital bed, who wouldn't?"

"After all," she said, "statistics say about a third of all people who have a mini-stroke have a major one within a year."

"Not an uplifting statistic." Mitch shook his head. "On the bright side, though, two-thirds of them don't have a major one."

"But who knows which side they're on until it happens? Take my mother. She had three mini-strokes before the big one took her down." Marla fussed with her blanket. "It really gets a person thinking."

"About?"

"Life."

"What about it?"

"Well, look at *your* life, Mitch. Or Grace's and Jesse's. Or Suzanne's and Rob's. Even Rachel's. Every one of you—you all have some kind of spiritual side going on."

"It's like a void in your life, isn't it, when you don't truly know the Lord?"

She nodded. "There's a difference. I can see it now. Maybe it's because I'm bumping up against sixty or spending the night in a hospital. Anyway, I want to change my life. I'm tired of living this way."

"Tired of living what way?" He raised an eyebrow.

"Focused on money. Clawing my way to my goals. Constant striving."

"How would you rather live your life?

"I want ... peace." She paused. "And when I die—which could have easily happened tonight—I want to be sure I'm going to heaven."

Mitch's eyes widened. "I see." He nodded. "Well, I think you're ready."

"For heaven? Or to die?"

"To ask Jesus to be Lord of your life." A hopeful but serious look crossed Mitch's face, like she had finally said something he'd been waiting to hear.

"I never heard it put that way."

"That's understandable. Every denomination has their own words to describe salvation. Your parents were Catholic, right?"

'Tis the Time,' 'Tis the Season

"My mom was Roman Catholic and my dad, Greek Catholic."

"Understanding salvation in your own heart and mind, that's all that matters." Mitch smiled. "You said you want to know for sure that when you die, you'll end up in heaven. In other words, that you're saved. Did I get that right?"

Marla suddenly felt like she was back in high school, hearing nuns and priests talking about heaven and salvation. She'd scoffed at their beliefs back then, but over the years, she'd wondered how much they'd said was true, and right now, every word of it finally made sense.

"That's right. Heaven. I want to end up in heaven. Hopefully, it won't be anytime soon, though." Marla smiled sheepishly.

Mitch's face lit up as he looked deeply into her eyes. "All right, then, I'd like you to repeat this prayer after me ..."

As Mitch spoke, Marla repeated his words. She understood what she was saying, and she meant it too. Her voice may have sounded emotional, yet a new kind of peace settled into her heart, like she'd crossed over a bridge to a different life, to a new and better way of living.

After they said *amen*, Mitch looked her in the eye. "Now, keep praying every day, read your Bible, and get yourself to church every Sunday."

"Maybe I could go to your church?" She'd been to his Assembly of God church before, so it seemed like the best choice.

"Sure." Mitch reached for her hand. "You know, I've prayed the sinner's prayer many a time in prisons but never bedside in a hospital and never with someone I cared about so deeply." His looked at her with beseeching eyes.

Marla's breath caught. Mitch cared for her deeply? She was not the only one with those thoughts? She opened her mouth but didn't know what to say. She held onto his hand and looked into his eyes, searching for an explanation of what was going on with them.

Marla continued her gaze, but neither of them spoke. The sounds from hospital equipment and voices in the hall filled the vacuum.

"There's her room!" Jesse's voice carried from outside the room, interrupting the moment.

"We'll finish this conversation later," Mitch said, patting her hand.

She had no doubt.

Grace rushed in, her arms reaching out to Marla, and Jesse ambling behind her. "Oh, my goodness, how are you doing?" Concern was written all over her face. Poor Grace, she'd lost both her adoptive parents in the past year. She didn't need to lose her birth mother too.

"Don't worry, I'm fine." Marla glanced at Mitch. "Even better than fine. Good as new." Marla lifted her left arm, made a fist, then opened the hand wide. "See, everything's back to normal."

"Grace, you can stop worrying." Jesse stood at the foot of the bed with his hands in his pockets, like he didn't know what to do with them.

"I'll be back home tomorrow." At least Marla hoped so.

"But I'll take care of you for a while, okay?" Grace reached for her mother's hand.

"That would be wonderful." Marla smiled at Grace then slipped a wink to Mitch.

Chapter 50

SUZANNE

Suzanne padded downstairs around nine in the morning, wondering how she hadn't heard Rob getting out of bed before her. She found him in the kitchen, already dressed and sitting at the table with his laptop, humming.

Rob never hummed.

"Good morning, sweetheart." She leaned over and kissed him.

"It's a good morning, indeed. Busy too." He continued humming.

"What are you working on?" Suzanne squinted at his computer screen. "I don't have my reading glasses with me. What's it say?"

"This is the to-do list for my practice. All the steps I'll need to expand."

It looked like a reasonably long list, but Suzanne had no idea what it said.

"I'll have to jump through some hoops to get licensed in Pennsylvania, but I can handle that."

He clicked to another document. "And this is your consignment sales agreement. After we discussed it last night, I figured I'd finalize it for you."

"Oh my gosh, what a darling you are. I meant to get up early so I'd have time to finish, and here you've already done it for me."

He clicked once again. "And this, my dear, is *la pièce de résistance*."

How she loved it when he spoke in French. Such a romantic language. She squeezed his bicep in excitement and leaned over the screen. "What is it?"

It was a picture of Mary Frances's house on Hilltop Lane. "Is that her listing?" Suzanne asked, curious.

"Yes," Rob said. "But I think she might already have an offer," Rob said.

"Wonder who's buying it." Suzanne took a step toward the coffee machine.

"Key's under the front door mat." Rob's voice had a smile in it.

"Huh?" Suzanne's face contorted in confusion.

"Get dressed," he said, laughing. "Let's go see our new house."

"What are you talking about?" She still couldn't follow him.

"I talked with Mary Frances about twenty minutes ago. She hasn't put her house up for sale yet, but she's open to an offer—and she's willing to delay the closing until we sell the house in California." He closed his laptop and stood. "Let's go, girl!"

Suzanne couldn't recall a time she'd gotten dressed so fast. She and Rob were on Hilltop Lane within minutes. They dashed to the front door like two crazy kids.

Rob beat her to the welcome mat. He held up the key. "Would you like to do the honors?"

Chapter 51

RACHEL

Rachel's first order of business today was church. Not for Mass, but for confession.

She never liked going to confession, but the nuns had insisted on it every Friday. Like mandatory Sunday Mass, Friday confession had become her habit. Even after she was married, she continued to go, but since Stan died, she only went when she felt guilty about something.

Like now.

Rachel could feel the sweat in her armpits as she waited her turn inside the dark confessional. She shook her top to let her skin breathe, then took a few breaths herself.

The voice in the other booth subsided, and a moment later, Father Obringer opened the window to Rachel's side.

She made the sign of the cross. "Bless me, Father, for I have sinned." She dropped her voice low and wondered if he'd still recognize her. Didn't matter. He'd piece things together soon enough. "My last confession was about nine months ago, around Easter."

After that, what an earful she gave him. Pride. Prejudice. Judgmentalism. Selfishness. Lust. Lies. Envy. Anger. And all the details that went with every sin.

When she finally exhausted her list, the priest absolved her from her sins and told her to say five *Our Fathers*—and not to wait so long for her next confession.

She exited the booth, feeling like a load had been taken from her, even though she knew she had some humbling conversations ahead.

Pete was first on her list. Ever since he'd told her about Lindsey's pregnancy, he'd made himself scarce. No wonder. What man in his thirties wants to listen to his mother preaching to him about sex before marriage? Pete didn't need her butting into his life or judging him. She was no saint herself.

She drove straight from church to Food 'n Fuel, hoping she could catch him when he wasn't busy. After she parked behind the building, she sat still for a while, asking God for the right words to say to her son—as well as to everyone else she owed an apology.

Chapter 52

MARLA

"Your discharge papers are almost ready," said the nurse in a chipper voice. "You might want to call your ride to come get you."

"Already?" Marla looked at the clock. It was barely the middle of the morning.

"You don't want to stay any longer, do you?" The nurse teased before scooting out of Marla's room.

An early discharge? Who could explain it? Whatever the reason, Marla was happy to get out of there and even happier Mitch would be picking her up.

She slipped into the outfit she'd been wearing yesterday and took a seat to wait for him. Last time she spent the night in a hospital was more than two years ago, back when she was in a relationship with a guy named Todd. What had she ever seen in him?

For that matter, what had she ever seen in Warren? She'd been so carried away with her list of what she wanted in a man, she failed to realize the list had become out of date.

"Good morning," Mitch said, all smiles, as he stepped inside the hospital room. "Ready to blow this joint?"

"Let's get out of here." She grabbed his arm with one hand and her purse with the other.

They sauntered toward the elevator, arms looped. Had they just become a couple? *Nah, don't be absurd, too soon for that.* She stole a sideways glance at Mitch. If not yet a couple, they were on their way there. She felt it inside and could see it in his smile.

"Hold on a moment," came a stern voice from the nurses' station. Carol Ann, the nurse from the zoning meeting, rolled out a wheelchair. "I'll take you downstairs in this."

Marla balked. She didn't want to let go of Mitch.

"Hospital rules." Standing wide, Carol Ann crossed her scrawny arms.

"Aw, c'mon, Carol Ann." Mitch waved a hand. "You know I'll get Marla out of here safely."

Carol sighed then chuckled, as if she'd broken this rule more than once. "Okay, Mitch, you can push her out. Leave the wheelchair in the lobby."

Grinning, he wheeled Marla into the elevator. "Your driver will get you home in a jiffy."

"If you've got time," Marla said, looking up, "there's something I'd like to talk with you about. Can we stop somewhere quiet?"

Mitch raised an eyebrow. "Hm. I think I can make that work." He pulled out his phone and sent a text to rearrange his morning. "How about the riverwalk?"

"Perfect."

Once they got into Mitch's truck, Marla read her discharge instructions aloud. "No smoking, no drinking, no drugs, eat healthy, exercise, maintain proper weight, take prescribed medications." She moaned. "I'm already doing all of that."

"Sure you are, but even so, it's up to the Lord when he wants to call you home."

'Tis the Time, 'Tis the Season

"I know that."

She remained silent until they reached the river. As Mitch pulled into a parking space, she watched some ducks contentedly bobbing up and down on the water. Such simple lives. Such short lives—at least compared to humans. "It's just ... it's just that I know my end could be soon. I want to make the most of every day."

Mitch turned off the ignition. "I know what you mean. I feel the same way."

She turned quickly. "You don't have something wrong with you, do you?" Her world was finally focused on the right priorities, and that world included Mitch.

"My health is fine," he said. "What I mean is, everyone's time on earth is limited. We all should make the most of every day." He looked at her, his eyes intense. "You know you'll get to heaven one day, right?"

"Right."

"But if you want to have joy and peace the rest of your days on this earth—if you want everything the Lord has for you—you have to surrender your life to him."

"Surrender?" An image of her holding a white flag came to Marla's mind.

"Yes. Give up your life to gain everything that's important. God will guide you all the way, if you just give up control."

Marla fell silent for a few moments. She remembered Aunt Adele saying Grace was losing her life to save it. Now, the words made sense.

"You can't just snap your fingers or say a quick prayer to make it happen," Mitch said. "It's more like a discipline, where you make that promise of surrender to the Lord over and over, and one day, you realize you really mean it. Believe me, it changes everything. It turns your daily existence into an exciting adventure."

She dropped her chin. "So, I've been living my life wrong all these years?"

"Don't be hard on yourself, Marla. No one starts out with a surrendered life, and most people never get to where you are right now. Pray about it and God will guide you, okay?"

She nodded. "I will."

They sat still a while, not talking, just absorbing the moment.

Surrender. She wanted to do it. She said a silent prayer to yield her life to God, knowing she'd probably have to pray it again tomorrow. And the next day. And the next.

Her thoughts turned to Grace. Mitch. Suzanne. Rachel. God had put all of them into her life for his purposes.

Maybe even a thrilling adventure.

She reached into her plastic discharge bag and pulled out one of the magazines Mitch had bought her. "Look at this." She showed him the cover. "Could you and your men build a house like this?"

"A tiny house?" Mitch took the magazine and flipped pages to the story inside. He rubbed his chin while looking at the pictures. "Nothing all that difficult here. Sure, we could do that—but that's a pretty radical downsizing." He looked up. "I don't know if the Lord would immediately ask you to surrender both your Manhattan condo and the spa."

"Oh, I agree he's not." Marla's eyes sparkled.

Mitch smacked himself on his forehead. "Ah, I get it. This is your new idea for the foster kids, isn't it?"

"Yes. Imagine this—a community of tiny houses built on my land, owned or rented by young people who have aged out of foster care—as well as anyone who wants the simplicity and the low cost of living in a small space with no steps."

"Houses with no steps? Hmm. So you're talking about Port Mariette's senior citizens, I presume?"

"Exactly. Lots of older people here can't safely live in a house with steps, which is pretty much every house in this town. If they can't afford to move to Sunset Hills, they either turn their living room into their bedroom or move in with their kids. Not the best options."

"I'm following." Mitch nodded.

Marla shifted herself to the edge of the seat. "Imagine this—a development of maybe a hundred tiny houses, complete with sidewalks, bike paths, a dog park, a community room, a fitness center—"

"Where would people park their cars?"

"Could you attach a one-car garage to the house?"

"I don't see why not."

Marla leaned in toward Mitch. "So you can definitely do this project?"

"Me? Well, I'd have to round up a lot of subcontractors, but sure."

"Great!"

"First, though, there are a lot of state regulations to look into, and after that, you'd have to get past those obstinate PMBA members, to say nothing of Fred with all his building codes, and most of all, Penny. She may be strange, but in this town, she's a force."

"I know," Marla said. "Lots of details to consider." She smiled knowingly at him. "But when God guides you to it—"

Mitch finished the sentence. "He'll get you through it."

Chapter 53

SUZANNE

Just as Suzanne turned the key to unlock Mary Frances's house, Rob put his arm between her and the door.

"Before we go inside, there's something you should know."

Suzanne sighed. "Okay, what's the bad news?"

"Mary Frances is selling the house *as is*. She doesn't want the hassle of having the house inspected."

"What if there's something major wrong with it, like a bad furnace or termites?

"We can still have the house inspected—she just won't fix anything. So our offer should reflect what we think the value of the house is based on what we learn in our inspection."

"We'll have to find a good home inspector." She squinted in thought. "Mitch is the only person around here I'd trust to give us an honest inspection."

"I wonder if he can inspect the house for mine subsidence too," Rob said.

Suzanne raised an eyebrow. "How did you know about mine subsidence?"

"Look, Suzanne, I got burned over ground movement. I won't let that happen again."

"I don't think you have to worry about falling into the ocean," she said. "This house overlooks the river, not the side of a cliff."

"But there are mines running beneath this entire valley. We need to make sure there's no mine subsidence that's already occurred." Clearly Rob had done some research.

"And after that, we'll buy mine subsidence insurance?" Suzanne raised an eyebrow to question him.

"Of course." Rob nodded. "There's one more thing I should mention before we go inside."

"What's that?" Suzanne's voice now had a note of exasperation. What else was there to talk about?

"I hope you like Mary Frances's decorating style." Rob grimaced.

Suzanne snorted. "I doubt I will—but the furnishings don't matter, just the house itself."

"Actually, you might care a lot," he said. "Not only is Mary Frances selling the house as is, she's also selling it furnished. Apparently, her furniture's not right for Florida." He shrugged. "We're stuck with whatever's in there."

"Seriously?" Suzanne couldn't imagine how Mary Frances, lover of polyester clothing and cheap jewelry, might have decorated this home. She sighed, deflated. "Oh, well, let's get this over with."

She pushed her way inside and immediately let out a loud gasp. Everywhere she looked, she loved what she saw. "This furniture is all Late Baroque—can you believe it?" She got down on her knees to examine it.

"I don't even know what *Early* Baroque furniture looks like. But whatever you call it, every piece seems perfect for this house. Very elegant."

"I think some of it might even be antique. Look at these dovetail joints."

Rob joined her on the floor. "I had no idea you were a furniture expert."

"I used to go to museums with my flight attendant friend, Barbara, when we were stuck somewhere for a weekend. She was a collector." Suzanne got back on her feet and looked around the living room. "She'd go nuts over this furniture."

"You mean you'd want to sell it to her?"

"Oh, never! Our California furniture would look ridiculous here. Every piece here is perfect for this home." Suzanne was half-way into the kitchen when she finished the sentence. "A renovated kitchen—can you believe it?" She pulled open drawers and cabinets, a grin wide across her face. "And what a view of the river from the breakfast nook!"

"Let's check out the bedroom," Rob said with that sexy laugh she loved.

She ran upstairs with Rob nipping at her heels, trying to grab her from behind.

They entered three bedrooms before finding the luxurious master bedroom.

"I've always wanted a four-poster bed." Suzanne turned to Rob, looking like a little girl hoping to fulfill her heart's desire.

He pulled her onto the bed with him. Their bodies tangled, they kissed and snuggled, then turned flat on their backs. "So you really love it?" Rob asked.

"Antique furniture, velvet upholstery, oriental carpets, renovated kitchen, and a four-poster bed? What's not to love? But now, the question is, can we afford it? The house alone would be expensive enough. With these furnishings included, I just don't know."

"All we can do is call Mary Frances and see." He reached for his phone.

Suzanne put her hand on Rob's arm. "How about if I call her?"

"You want to call Mary Frances?" Rob looked incredulous.

Surely Mary Frances couldn't be harder to deal with than Sharon at Hair & Care. Suzanne nodded, a sly smile on her face. "Lately, I've been learning a lot about how to close a deal."

Chapter 54

RACHEL

Rachel left work early so she'd have time to make Tony his favorite meal, a spicy sausage lasagna. She hummed nervously as she removed the aluminum foil and tested it with a fingertip. A few more minutes in the oven, then she'd let it rest until he arrived.

The doorbell rang and she hurried to let him in. He looked her up and down. "Wow. You look terrific. Did you get all dressed up just for me?" He laughed as he wrapped his arms around her and gave her a kiss. "And do I smell your spicy sausage lasagna?" He sniffed loudly.

"Yes, you do, and it's almost ready." She gave him a peck on the cheek. "Open a bottle of wine for yourself and take a seat."

He went to the table, a single wineglass on it. "No wine for you?"

"Not tonight." She pulled the lasagna from the oven and brought the bread and salad into the dining room.

"Yum." Tony's eyes twinkled as he reached for the fresh Italian bread.

Rachel raised a hand to stop him. "How about we say grace for a change?"

"Okay." Tony put the bread down. You wanna say it?"

"Sure." She made the sign of the cross. "Bless us, O Lord, and these thy gifts, which we are about to receive from thy bounty, through Christ our Lord. Amen."

"Haven't heard that in a while." Tony looked at her sheepishly. "We should do that with every meal." He bit into his buttered bread.

"We should."

She went to the kitchen, returning with two heavy plates of steaming lasagna.

"This is really great," Tony said, digging in. "You're the best cook in the world."

Rachel beamed. Stan had never complimented her cooking. Well, once, when they were first married, but never after that.

"We're really good for each other, aren't we?" Tony said, reaching for her hand.

Rachel squirmed and pulled back her hand. "After I tell you what happened last night, you might not think so." She recounted her accident for him, not leaving out a single detail. Tony had almost finished his meal when she finally finished her monologue. She held her breath, waiting for his reaction to her confession.

"Got any more lasagna?" was all he said.

Rachel giggled. After everything she'd just told him, that wasn't what she'd been expecting. She took his plate into the kitchen and cut him another square.

"Thanks," Tony said, his fork waiting upright in his hand.

"I feel so bad about the way I've been behaving," Rachel said, half her meal still on her plate. "Not just about the August Village kids. That's a big part of it, but not the whole story. I've been so full of myself lately with becoming PMBA

'Tis the Time,' Tis the Season

president and bragging about you. I hurt my relationship with both Suzanne and Marla." She shook her head and sighed. "I've been so blind."

Tony took a sip of wine. "Well, bragging about me, I could understand." He winked, then he turned serious. "Look, Rachel. You've been going through some rough times. Lots of pressure on you at PMBA. The Christmas parade's around the corner. Pete's big wedding has turned into a civil ceremony, and a grandkid's already on the way. As for that accident, I blame myself as much as you. I never should have allowed you to drive home after drinking. So give yourself a break. Honestly, I don't know how you do it all." He shook his head. "And look at this meal. Wow. In my book, you're an amazing woman."

She had to hand it to him, Tony did know how to make her feel better. "Thank you. That's nice of you to say. I think you're pretty amazing too."

"Y'know, when two people each think the other one is amazing, sometimes they do something about it. Like, they get married. What do you think about that, Rachel? I don't know about you, but I've been thinking about it for a while, and seeing you so sweet and vulnerable here tonight really touched my heart. I do think you're an amazing woman, and I would be honored if you'd be my wife."

Rachel's hand flew to her heart. A proposal was something she certainly had not expected. What should she say? She had to say something. Tony was waiting, and his face looked so hopeful. Did she love him? She enjoyed his company, and they had a lot in common—but love him? Or love him enough to spend the rest of her life with him? Such a big question, one she was unprepared to answer.

She reached for his hand, kissed it tenderly. "Oh, Tony. You are so sweet. You came into my life at the right time, when I needed you most. You brought me laughter, joy, comfort, companionship—well, I could go on, but you get the drift. You know I'm nuts about you."

"So you wanna get married?" He grinned widely.

"I think I would like to marry you—but I'm not ready." She said it softly, not wanting to hurt him. "I still have a lot of repair work to do—with Pete and Lindsey, with my friends, throughout the whole town, in fact. Stan died less than two years ago, you know. I've still got some learning and growing to do before I'm ready to be a wife again. Next time—if there is a next time, that is—I want to be a better wife too."

Tony looked so deflated. "You're not closing the door, are you?"

"Not at all. For now, though, let me work on myself a while."

"Okay, sweetie. I'll be right here waiting." Tony pulled her on his lap.

"I'm counting on that." Rachel hugged him tight and kissed him long.

Chapter 55

MARLA

To Marla's delight, Grace *adored* the tiny homes idea, so she called Mitch to brainstorm about next steps. She also hoped to discuss something else weighing on her mind.

"Why don't you put on a coat," Mitch said, "and I'll pick you up in a half hour. We can go back to the riverwalk and get some fresh air. It'll do you good."

Soon they were leaning over the railing of Port Mariette's bridge. Although Mitch was close by her side, and they were supposed to be planning the tiny homes development, her mind was stuck on something else.

"Can I ask you a question?" Marla looked up at Mitch's rugged face, feeling sure he'd know the answer.

"You can ask me anything." Smiling, he glanced at her from the corner of his eye. "Might not answer you, though."

"Ha, ha, very funny." She paused. "Listen, I've been playing back some conversations in my mind. It's helping me understand some things I didn't catch the first time around."

"Like what?"

"Like when Grace told me about the guy she was dating in high school, who she really liked. It was Jesse, wasn't it?"

Mitch looked into her eyes but didn't answer.

"And you also know why they stopped seeing one another, don't you?"

He pursed his lips.

"And Jesse's father was a horrible man."

Mitch still hadn't said a word. No matter. The expression on his face was all the confirmation she needed. How could she have missed all of Grace's clues?

No wonder Grace and Jesse were drawn together so quickly when he moved back to town. Why they wanted children. Why they both yearned to help young people. Why the thought of telling his father his girlfriend was pregnant terrified Jesse.

"Their baby would have been a young adult now," Marla softly said.

Mitch nodded.

"Jesse told you everything while he was in that West Virginia prison, didn't he?"

"Yep."

"And that's why you've been so supportive of him and Grace, isn't it?

"Jesse's one of the top people on my list. Grace too." He put his arm around Marla and pulled her close. "You, my dear, are even higher on that list."

She didn't know what to say. Instead, she stared at the river, glistening as it ran under the bridge.

"Don't hold that abortion against him," Mitch said. "He was young and scared."

"I know. I'm not holding it against Grace, so why would I hold it against Jesse? He may have paid for it, but Grace agreed to go through with it."

Mitch put both his elbows on the railing and joined her in looking at the river below. "We all have regrets from our youth."

'Tis the Time, 'Tis the Season

"You too?" She twisted her head to look at him. "You have regrets?" He'd never mentioned any to her.

Mitch nodded. "I spent a year fooling around in Pittsburgh when I was young. Made a lot of mistakes with women and drinking, ended up in a hospital."

"So you do have some regrets." Marla said it softly, knowing she had plenty of her own.

"Only a fool wouldn't have any," he said. "Lucky I didn't land in a jail cell."

"Hard to imagine you there." She looked up at him. "Is that how you got involved with prison ministry?"

"Eventually. First, I had to figure a few things out, like why I was still alive." His eyes got a faraway look. "There was a guy who used to stand on Fifth and Smithfield up in Pittsburgh handing out Gospel tracts. I always avoided him, but after I got out of the hospital, I went straight there to find him."

Mitch grinned. "The guy nearly talked my ear off, but at some point, I finally understood what he was saying. Right then and there, I decided God wanted me to use the abilities he'd given me to fulfill my purpose on this earth."

"Such a powerful story."

"Oh, there's more. I knew I had to get out of Pittsburgh, otherwise I'd get off track again. So I moved back to Port Mariette and started doing the only constructive thing I knew how to do—which, ironically, turned out to be construction."

"So your work is your purpose? Like, maybe my foundation might be my purpose now?"

"Could be. You have to figure this stuff out on your own. For me, starting a general contracting business was just the beginning of my new life. I had to *work out my salvation*, as Paul called it in the Bible."

"How did you do that?"

"Worked hard. Prayed harder. Stayed away from women."

"All these years?" Marla could hardly believe a man like Mitch didn't have plenty of opportunities.

"Until now." He gave her a squeeze.

More people flowed onto the bridge, talking and laughing.

"C'mon," Mitch said. "Let's go sit on one of those benches. Too many eyes, too many ears on the bridge this evening." He settled his hand on her waist and led her to an empty bench.

She took a seat near the middle so Mitch's body would have to touch hers. How comfortable she felt being close to him.

He stretched an arm across the back of the bench, just like he'd done that day at the arts festival when she and Warren were walking along Main Street.

"I have regrets too," Marla said, almost a whisper. "Not just from my younger days, in fact. Even now."

"How so?"

"I think you know what I mean. I wasted a lot of my life on the wrong people, the wrong places, the wrong goals. I practically had to die in order to realize what I was doing."

"At least you realized it. Some people never do." He hugged her shoulder. "I realized something the moment I met you. Do you remember the first day you came to town, when you were buying groceries for your aunt at the Dairy Mart?"

She nodded, a smile on her face. It was spring last year. She'd told everyone she'd come early for the reunion so she could look in on Aunt Adele, but her real reason was that she wanted to find her daughter.

"Of course I remember," she said. "That's when you told me I looked like a swan in a coal mine."

'Tis the Time,' Tis the Season

"It was the first thing that came to my mind." He shrugged. "A little odd, I guess, but you had me gobsmacked." He laughed at his own choice of words. He pulled her closer to him. "You knocked me out that day. You still do."

Marla's breath caught. His words, so unique, so genuine—they touched her heart.

"I couldn't get you out of my mind after that. I still can't. At first, I thought it was because you stood out so much in this town with your expensive jewelry and fancy clothes. Or because you're so beautiful." He squeezed her again. "But then we worked together on the spa renovation, and I got to know you. I realized there was a lot more to you than jewels and money. You're a complex lady, you know that?" He smiled as he lifted her chin toward him for a second.

"So I've been told."

"How many times I wanted to tell you how I felt about you, but I couldn't. Warren was always in the picture. When you told me you and Warren were done, you can understand why I jumped in right away."

"Glad you did."

"I don't want to pressure you, Marla, but I want you to know how I feel. I realize you and I are as different as Manhattan and Port Mariette. Even so, I've seen you changing, and I care for you more than ever. Now, it's up to you, whether or not you want to do anything about it."

She didn't know what to say, so instead of babbling, she looked away, as if the river or sky could give her the words.

He took her hand and kissed it. "Enough of that mushy stuff. Let's talk about those tiny homes."

He looked a little sad that she hadn't committed to anything, but what could she say? She was still figuring things out herself.

Chapter 56

SUZANNE

Suzanne swooshed into her mother's room at Sunset Hills just as the sun was setting. "In the mood for a surprise?" Bubbling with joy, Suzanne wasn't sure what to say first.

"Always." Her mother pushed a button to aright her recliner. "You know I love a surprise as much as you do."

Suzanne plopped into the chair next to her mother. "Jill's pregnant!"

"Oh, my goodness, how wonderful." Her mother's hand flew to her mouth. "Elizabeth will grow up with a sibling, just like you and Andrea."

Suzanne nodded excitedly. "And there's even more news."

"Twins?" Her mother's eyes widened.

Suzanne laughed at the thought. With Elizabeth not yet a toddler, Jill would have her hands full with even one more baby. "No, not that."

She moved to the edge of her chair to get closer. "Take a look at these pictures." Suzanne clicked open her phone.

"That's one of the houses on Millionaire's Row, isn't it?" her mother asked.

Suzanne quivered with excitement. "Yes. It's Mary Frances's house. She's moving to Florida, and guess what, Rob and I are buying it!"

"What? You're moving back to Port Mariette? Omigosh, I don't know what to say. I'm overwhelmed." Suzanne's mother dabbed her eyes with a fingertip. "I didn't even know you were thinking of moving back here."

"It all happened suddenly. Because of that insurance issue."

"That house is gorgeous, but you don't have to spend all that money to buy Mary Frances's house. You and Rob could live in my house instead. It would save you a mountain of money."

"That's sweet of you, Mom. Thanks. If it were just me, that would be great, but I need an art studio, and Rob will be working out of the house, so he'll need space too. Besides, he loves that view overlooking the river."

"Well, as long as you're in Port Mariette, that's all that matters to me." She couldn't hold back the tears any longer. "And two great-grandchildren only an hour away. It's almost more than my heart can hold." She reached for a tissue.

"I feel the same way," Suzanne said, taking a tissue for herself. "Just wait till you see this house. Mary Frances is selling it with all the furnishings, and they are perfect." She put her phone down and blotted her eyes. "Want to go see it tomorrow morning? I could pick you up around nine-thirty. Rachel invited me and Marla to lunch at noon, so that should be more than enough time."

"I'll be ready." Her mom grinned. "And once you buy that house, remember to get mine subsidence insurance."

Chapter 57

RACHEL

Rachel bustled about in the overheated kitchen, putting together the oddest lunch she'd made in quite a while—spanakopita and airplane chicken. She wiped her forehead with the back of her hand as she opened the kitchen door and let Cinders out.

The spanakopita was in honor of Marla's Greek heritage, and the chicken breast with its leg attached was supposed to resemble a plane, in honor of Suzanne's long career in the airline industry.

The last time she'd made these two dishes was when Suzanne and Marla came to town for their high school reunion. Rachel hoped serving a nostalgic meal would get her back in their good graces.

Heck, if things went well, Suzanne and Marla might even agree to help with the Christmas parade, now only days away. Rachel still didn't have enough people committed to participate. Who would bother watching a parade consisting of only Santa and a small marching band?

A car door slammed outside. Noon on the dot. Rachel wiped her jittery hands on a dish towel and hurried to the front door to greet Suzanne and Marla, coming up the porch steps.

"You're here!" Rachel put her hands together, as if she were praying. And why shouldn't she? Their willingness to come here was an answer to her prayers. She waved them both inside but didn't touch them, suspecting a hug might be rebuffed. "It's so good to see you both."

As Marla took a seat on one end of the sofa, Rachel looked her over. As far as she could tell, Marla looked fine. Her mouth moved normally, she was using both arms, and she wasn't slurring any words. Thank goodness. If that stroke had been a serious one, Rachel could never forgive herself for contributing to Marla's stress.

"I remember the first time we got together here," Marla said, looking around the room. "I brought a bottle of champagne in my purse." She glanced at Suzanne, now sitting on the other end. "Remember?"

"Who could forget?" Suzanne chortled.

"Well, look what I just found." Marla opened her bag and pulled a magnum of champagne from it.

Rachel sucked in a breath. Was Marla crazy? She knows she shouldn't be drinking.

"Wipe that worried look off your face." She handed Rachel the bottle. "It's nonalcoholic. I have no idea if it tastes any good, but let's give it a whirl."

Relieved, Rachel returned with wine glasses. Last year, they'd used beer glasses. "I still don't have champagne glasses, but I did get a few wine glasses." She didn't dare mention Tony had bought them for her. Last thing she wanted to do was agitate Suzanne.

Rachel placed the wine glasses on the table and sat on the upholstered chair across from the sofa.

Marla filled three glasses with the fake champagne. "Looks like ginger ale." She made a face then raised her glass. "To our health."

What a relief Marla had given a toast they could all agree on.

Rachel took a sip. Not bad. She took another sip and put her glass back on the table.

"Before we do anything else, I need to apologize to both of you." Rachel cleared her throat. "I've been behaving like such a jerk. I hope you can forgive me." She winced at the awkwardness of it all. "I got caught up in my own self-importance at PMBA and didn't bother to keep both of you in the loop. Suzanne, I should have let you know about retail space opening up, and I shouldn't have gone overboard talking about Tony. That was insensitive of me."

"Thank you for saying that, Rachel, but I'm the one who owes you an apology. If anyone's been a jerk, it's me." Suzanne touched her chest. "I've been so on edge. I'm sorry I overreacted." She smiled. "I do have a tendency to do that. Can you forgive me?"

"Of course I can." Rachel said it with conviction. "But I was wrong, and you called me out on it. I needed that."

She turned to Marla. "And speaking of overreacting—Marla, I overreacted about your proposal for the spa. I was so caught up in taking care of the town's business interests that I forgot about taking care of human beings. Those kids at August Village have a tough enough life without me making it harder. Can you forgive me for trying to turn everyone against your project?"

"Sure I can." Marla said, her eyes twinkling. "My plans have changed, anyway."

"Really?" Rachel knit her brows. Was another battle on the horizon?

"Don't worry," Marla quickly added. "I think the entire town will like my new proposal. Grace and Jesse are already on board, and Mitch has agreed to oversee the construction."

Rachel's mouth dropped open. "Construction?"

Chapter 58

MARLA

"Yes, construction." Marla reached into her tote bag and pulled out a rolled-up sheet of paper. "This is very rough, but it'll give both of you an idea of what I'm talking about." She moved to the center of the sofa next to Suzanne and waved Rachel over. "Come sit over here so you can see."

"The spa is located here." Marla pointed to a square on the left side of the map. "Most of the land, about fifty acres, is to its right. I never use any of these acres, other than taking an occasional walk or having a picnic."

"A picnic?" Rachel giggled. "I can't imagine you on a picnic, Marla."

Marla shrugged. "You know me, always full of surprises." She traced her finger along a line meandering throughout her property in a wavy circle. "Imagine this road winding its way through the open spaces. With all these curves, the road will be visually appealing, and it will reduce the need for cutting down trees."

Rachel and Suzanne both stared silently at the drawing, so Marla continued. "Now, let me ask you a question," she said. "Are you familiar with tiny houses?" She pulled a magazine from her tote and showed them the cover.

"Oh, yes. They're so adorable." Suzanne put a hand on her heart. "Of course, I wouldn't want to live in one of them. I'd get claustrophobic."

"Can I see that magazine?" Rachel flipped to the article inside.

"What are they, a couple hundred square feet?" Suzanne asked.

"It varies," Marla said. "Some are really small, maybe a little more than two hundred square feet, and others a few hundred more."

"Well, Rob and I both like a lot of space," said Suzanne. "Tiny homes are precious but not nearly enough space for two people."

Rachel kept flipping through the pages. "They remind me of my mom's ranch house in Florida. Small, but just enough space, and no steps. Very practical. Utilities would be a fraction of what she's paying on her air conditioning down there."

"Exactly." Marla said it with assurance. "Utility costs in tiny houses would be low. Same with maintenance costs."

"And like Suzanne said, they really are adorable." Smiling, Rachel gave the magazine back to Marla.

She'd captured Rachel's interest, so Marla continued. "Imagine a development of tiny homes, all of them with well-designed exteriors and with cement foundations, no basements."

"My mother used to do her laundry in her basement," Rachel said. "She was always afraid of falling on those rickety wooden steps."

"And usually basements are just a place to hold onto junk," Suzanne added.

"Exactly." Marla put her finger back on the drawing. "Imagine the homes built all along this road. Some of them will have an attached one-car garage, and others, just a

'Tis the Time, 'Tis the Season

driveway to park a car or two on. The sidewalks will be wide, with room for walking and for a bike path, and in the wooded areas, there will be hiking paths. See this big square?" Marla pointed to the center of the drawing. "There will be a community center here, with a gym and a big kitchen where people can make meals for groups, along with rooms for classes like yoga or tai chi, for guest speakers, or where clubs or groups of people can meet." A thought popped into her head. "Like for bingo."

"Bingo? I don't think St. Cyp's will want the competition." Rachel squinted.

"It was just a thought." Marla waited to see if more questions would surface.

Rachel folded her arms. "And how many of these homes are you proposing to build for foster kids?"

"Ten phases of ten homes, for a total of one hundred."

"Wow. That's a lot." Rachel pulled back.

"But here's the beauty of this plan." Marla spread her hands across the drawing. "This is creating a community for single people of all ages—foster kids who have aged out, widows and widowers, the elderly, singles, divorced people. In other words, anyone who wants to live alone but doesn't want a lot of maintenance, high utility costs, or steps. You need a lot of residents to create that kind of community."

"It looks like you've thought of everything." Suzanne's eyes were wide.

Rachel's face had gone blank, so Marla forged on. "The name of this development will be *Best Life Village*. Residents will live independently, but there will also be a true sense of community. I envision the older residents teaching the younger residents about life skills, hobbies, careers, whatever—and the older residents benefiting from the younger ones too. They could help older residents with everything from using technology to carrying groceries."

Suzanne kept nodding. "Living side by side like this, everyone will have the best of all worlds."

"I get it now." Rachel nodded too. "I love how you're making a community of all kinds of single people." Finally, enthusiasm surfaced in her voice.

"So, Rachel, are you on board with this plan?" Marla held up the drawing.

"Well—"

Sniffing, Suzanne interrupted Rachel. "Is something burning?"

"Oh my gosh, it's the spanakopita." Rachel jumped up and disappeared into the kitchen.

Chapter 59

SUZANNE

"Did you get to the spanakopita in time?" Suzanne called out to Rachel, banging around in the kitchen.

"I think so." Rachel giggled as she carried the hot steaming meals into the dining room. "Thanks to your nose, Suzanne."

"Aw, you made airplane chicken too." Suzanne tilted her head to the side, touched by Rachel's meal selection.

"I'll say the blessing." Marla mumbled, her eyes averted.

Suzanne's eyes widened. In all the meals they'd shared together, Marla had never done such a thing, not even once.

Marla took in a big breath then let it out as she prayed. "Thank you, Lord, for the friendship we three women share and for this special meal we're having together. We ask your blessing on our food, our friendship, and our conversation."

All three of them said *amen*, and then Suzanne couldn't help but comment. "I believe that's the first time I've heard you pray out loud, Marla."

Marla shrugged and smiled. "New leaf."

Suzanne cocked an eye at her. Could there be good coming out of Marla's second mini-stroke? After all, a new lease on life can change perspective quickly. "Good for you." She waited for Marla to say more, but she didn't.

"Speaking of a new leaf," Suzanne continued, "Rob and I are turning one over too. We've decided to sell our house in Carmel Highlands." She paused for dramatic effect. "And guess what, we're moving to Port Mariette—*and* we're buying Mary Frances's house on Hilltop Lane."

"That's some big news." Marla widened her eyes. "Congratulations."

"Yes, congratulations," Rachel said, "but I have to admit, I'm shocked. That's quite the transition for you—and even more for Rob."

Suzanne shrugged. "I'm sure there will be challenges, but we're used to them by now. Besides, we both know in our hearts it's the right thing to do."

"Well, then, good for you," Rachel said. "I'm thrilled you'll be living here permanently. Then it won't be so hard to get together."

"And I won't need you to keep me in the loop so much." Suzanne winked at Rachel.

"Right," Rachel said. "How about you, Marla? I guess you'll have to stay here a while too, right? Or at least visit a lot. I mean, assuming you move forward with your tiny houses."

A smile sneaked across Marla's face. "So, Rachel—you're saying you'll support the project?"

"How could I not?" Rachel lifted her hands, palms up, as if she were the picture of innocence. She turned to Suzanne. "When are you closing on Mary France's house?"

"As soon as we sell the house in California. It shouldn't take long, now that we can prove it's on stable ground."

"Mary Frances didn't even tell me she put her house on the market." Rachel looked miffed, then she giggled. "I guess this is how it feels when your friends don't keep you in the loop."

Suzanne laughed. "Actually, she never put it on the market. Rob just picked up the phone and called her about it."

"That's a great idea," Marla said, tapping her fingers on the table. "And I've got another one. Now that you're moving here, Suzanne, would you consider a part-time position? I'd like to draw on your artistic skills for Best Life Village."

"What did you have in mind?"

"We'll have to talk with Mitch about the specifics," Marla said, "but in general, you'd work on design and color schemes, inside and out."

Suzanne grabbed Marla's hand and shook it hard. "I'm in."

Chapter 60

RACHEL

The three women finished their lunch, but Rachel couldn't remember eating a single bite. The emotion of the day, coupled with Marla's and Suzanne's revelations, had consumed every drop of her energy. Maybe, at least, she'd be able to enjoy dessert.

"How about a piece of pie with a scoop of ice cream?" Rachel didn't wait for their answers. Both Marla and Suzanne would probably say they couldn't eat another thing, but Rachel had worked too hard on this latticed cherry pie to allow anyone to skip it.

She scurried into the kitchen and brought the desserts into the living room. "I cut the pieces kinda small but there's more if you want it."

"Looks scrumptious." Suzanne took her first bite. "Mmm."

"I think this is going to fill me up to my eyeballs." Marla put her hand across her forehead.

Rachel took her seat and picked up a fork. "By the way, Marla, I was talking with Penny this morning. She said she saw you and Mitch on the riverwalk yesterday."

Marla pressed her lips into a flat line. "That Penny. She's sure got her ear to the ground."

"You're lucky it was Penny, not Walt," Suzanne said. "Otherwise, it would be another headline story."

Marla shrugged. "Well, Mitch and I obviously have a lot to talk about these days."

"Penny said you were sitting very close together." Rachel stared at Marla, whose face gave nothing away.

"Oh." Suzanne's eyes widened. "It just dawned on me, you haven't said a word about Warren lately. Is everything okay with you two?"

"Actually ... it's not." Marla toyed with her silverware while Rachel exchanged glances with Suzanne.

Finally, Marla put the fork down. "It seems Warren has been seeing someone—a woman who lives down the hall from him."

"I'm so sorry." Suzanne touched Marla's arm. "You two seemed so ... compatible."

Rachel kept silent. She'd never cared much for Warren. Who'd want to be compatible with an uppity guy like him?

"Compatible?" Marla shrugged. "At one time, maybe we were. But people do change. There were clues I should have caught. Remember how livid Warren was in July, when I told him Grace needed me to stay here in Port Mariette a while longer? He couldn't grasp why I prioritized my one and only daughter over him."

"I remember that day," Rachel said. "He stormed out of the arts festival, right past my booth. Hardly said goodbye. Just a little wave." Staring at the ceiling, Rachel added, "Y'know, another thing I remember about that arts festival is Mitch. I remember seeing him sitting on the bench in front of the coffee shop, watching that scene Warren made. I wondered back then if Mitch had a thing for you."

'Tis the Time,' 'Tis the Season

"Well, apparently I was too blind to notice he's *had a thing* for me since I first came to town." Marla allowed a little smile.

"And now you have a thing for him?" Rachel leaned forward, grinning like a matchmaker who'd just put a couple together. "I mean, are you two in a relationship?"

"I guess you could say that," Marla said, a little sheepishly, "although in some ways, it already seems more than that, like we've been together a long time."

"Well, you two have spent a lot of time together, just not as a couple," Suzanne said.

"True," Marla said. "But I don't want to rush things. Remember, I've been single all my life, and for good reason." Marla glanced at Suzanne, then Rachel, an unlikely tentativeness on her face. "You know my history. I don't want to make any more big mistakes."

Rachel could sympathize. Would she be making a big mistake with Tony? How could she know for sure, one way or the other? She looked at Suzanne. "You and Rob got married pretty fast. How did you know you weren't making a mistake?"

"We dated for nine months, so it wasn't all that fast, but with my crazy travel schedule, that probably wasn't long enough." Suzanne dropped her voice. "Believe me, there have been times I've wondered if I made a mistake. Remember how we had to cancel our honeymoon? What a way to start a marriage. And we've had plenty of ups and downs since then." Suzanne laughed. "But I do love Rob to pieces, and honestly, I wouldn't change a thing."

"But ... but ..." Rachel sputtered. "How would ... how would Marla know if Mitch is the one?"

"I wish I could tell you," Suzanne said with a shrug, "but the truth is, matters of the heart defy explanation."

That answer didn't help Rachel at all.

Chapter 61

MARLA

December 24

Someone fired a shot in the air, jolting Marla in her folding chair and causing a few folks in the crowd along Main Street to cry out in surprise.

Next to her, Grace clapped her hands in excitement. "That's the signal for the start of the parade."

"Ah, Sergeant Dan must be thrilled," Marla said. "He got to fire his gun." Other than on a shooting range, parades were probably his only other chance to release a bullet.

Kids kept running into the street to find out what was coming their way, and on the sidewalks, people strained to see the parade participants gathering.

Rachel had promised this would be *a doozy of a parade*, especially since Christmas Eve would be unseasonably warm. Still, Marla had to wonder—other than nice weather, what could be so fabulous about a little parade that it would draw such a large crowd? Still wondering, she looked to the end of the street where the parade would soon start.

A second later, Mitch's dark green pickup appeared. He would lead the parade, that much Marla knew. Inching forward, Mitch tossed candy to the kids.

Marla stood and waved when he drove by, wishing she were in the passenger seat helping. After all, both her arms worked now. But Mitch thought doing so might be too much for her. He was being ridiculous, but his concern touched her, so she'd relented. He'd set up folding chairs for her and Grace instead.

Jesse sat in Marla's place, tossing candy from the passenger side. Made sense. Jesse would do anything for kids.

The pickup crept along. In its bed stood Suzanne and Rob, dressed as elves, singing Christmas carols. Who would have guessed they'd make such a wonderful singing duo? Or look so adorable in elf costumes? Marla waved to them too.

Behind the pickup came the St. Cyprian's Academy marching band, all twenty members wearing uniforms that looked the same as when Marla was in school, only faded. Clearly, her foundation would have to make a donation.

After the band came people with pets. As PMBA president, Rachel could have sat on the back of one of Pete's old convertibles and waved to the crowd like a local dignitary, but instead, she and her old dog Cinders sauntered along with all the other pet lovers. Most of the group walked dogs on leashes, but a few people carried cats in cages, and to the delight of the crowd, a little red-haired girl pulled a turtle in a wagon.

After the pets passed, a handful of daredevil boys zoomed around on skateboards and go-carts, followed by several gymnasts flipping their way along the parade route. After that came a man driving an old John Deere tractor and waving flags. A man on stilts, dressed as Uncle Sam, followed a safe distance behind.

In their wake, Inez appeared, dancing a hula. A few elderly women belly-danced behind her. All of the women and many in the crowd laughed until they cried.

Next, two teenage boys marched along, holding a brightly colored banner that read *August Village*. Several dozen young people followed behind the sign, dressed in an assortment of red and green clothing and not a few Santa caps. They handed out homemade ornaments while calling out, "Merry Christmas! Happy new year!"

Marla raised an eyebrow and looked at Grace. "Did you arrange that?"

Grinning, Grace nodded. "Aunt Sissy called me the other night, panicked that she didn't have enough people in the parade. I told her I could round up a group from August Village."

"Why didn't you tell me?"

"I know you like surprises." Grace stood and waved as they passed by. "That's Isaiah and Landon holding the banner. They're Jesse's apprentices."

Police cars followed next, their sirens wailing to prepare the crowd for the arrival of Santa. From atop a firetruck, Herbie's voice boomed over the loudspeakers as he patted his belly and waved a white-gloved hand. "Ho, ho, ho, Merry Christmas," he chanted.

"Who's standing next to him in the Mrs. Claus costume?" Marla, straining to see, asked her daughter.

Grace squinted. "I can't tell, either."

Once Santa and Mrs. Claus reached the other end of Main Street, firefighters helped them off the truck onto a stage in front of the bank. Kids of all ages gleefully lined up for their gifts.

Next to the platform, a hot chocolate stand, manned by August Village youth in their red-and-white Santa hats, suddenly had a long line of its own.

"I'm guessing you arranged that hot chocolate stand too?" Marla asked, eyes on Grace.

"Oh, no. That was Jesse's idea." Grace chuckled. "We thought it might ease the way for you at the next town meeting."

"You two are full of surprises." Marla laughed. "Good ones."

Such a clever way to prepare people's hearts. No matter what happened at the meeting, Marla would accept the outcome. Throughout this visit, her relationship with Grace had deepened significantly, and that had always been the goal.

Mitch and Jesse rounded the corner, the parade now over.

"Why didn't you toss some candy my way, Mitch?" Marla teased as she got out of her chair.

"Silly woman," he said. "You're already sweet enough, don't you know that?" He gave her waist a squeeze. "How are you feeling? Are you tired? Ready to go home? My truck's right over there. I can drive over and pick you up." He pointed down the side street.

"I'm not an invalid, you know." She winked at Grace as she hooked her arm in Mitch's.

"You two kids go along." Grace laughed. "We'll bring the chairs back in Jesse's truck.

Marla waved goodbye as she and Mitch headed to his pickup. He made a U-turn in the lot, and they drove off for the spa.

Mitch helped her out of the truck, although she didn't need it, and he held her hand as they ascended the steps to the front door. Inside, they went straight to the loveseat. It seemed only appropriate.

Mitch reached his arm around Marla and pulled her close to him.

Today, his scent was fresh, like soap. Different, but she still liked it.

'Tis the Time,' 'Tis the Season

"Can I ask you a question?" Marla asked.

"Anything."

"I know we talked about this already," Marla said, "but this summer, when you said you weren't involved with Kim Kryzwicki—"

"How come you're bringing that up again? I already told you, I gave her a couple golf lessons. That was it. Didn't you believe me?" He joked, squeezing her closer to him.

"Oh, I believed you. I was just wondering ..."

"About what?"

"About the day of the arts festival, when we were sitting together on that bench, and Warren arrived—then left."

"Uh-huh. What about it?"

"Since you weren't dating Kim, and if Warren hadn't come to town, and if we were sitting together on that bench without him interrupting us—what would you have said to me that day?"

"What would I have said?" He lifted her chin and rubbed his rough hand on her smooth cheek. "I would have said nothing."

"Nothing?"

"That's right."

"Why nothing?"

"I think you know I already had feelings for you."

"Well, then, why didn't you say something?"

"I wasn't ready, and you weren't, either."

"Are we ready now?"

"Let's see." He drew her lips to his and gently kissed her.

Chapter 62

SUZANNE

January 2

The administration building was filling up fast when Suzanne arrived with Rob. He placed his hand on the small of her back, and together they moved to the front of the room, passing by Herbie, then Rachel, both sitting on the ends of their rows.

"Where's Tony? Suzanne leaned over and asked Rachel.

She pursed her lips. "Up in Pittsburgh. With his son."

Suzanne looked at her with understanding eyes but had to keep moving. The meeting would be starting soon. They passed Grace and Jesse in the first row then slipped into two folding chairs on the other side of Marla and Mitch.

Standing at the lectern a couple of feet in front of them, a dour-looking Penny rapped her gavel to call the meeting to order. Was her holiday mood already gone?

Suzanne had urged Marla to ask for this town meeting to take place right after the new year, when the Christmas spirit would still be on everyone's mind. With Penny, and who knows how many others, still opposed to Best Life Village, they needed to capitalize on every possible advantage. Judging by Penny's expression, though, the strategy seemed to not have any effect, at least on her.

Penny looked around the room, waiting for everyone to get quiet. "Tonight would be a good night for burglars, wouldn't it, hee, hee?" Her snicker sounded sinister to Suzanne. "Sure looks like the whole town's here."

Nervous laughter rippled through the room.

Suzanne whispered to Rob, "Did you lock the doors?"

He nodded as he patted her hand. "Don't worry, sweetheart, all the doors are locked."

"Thank you all for coming," Penny said, her smile wide like a sleazy politician's. "I hope you had a wonderful Christmas and New Year's Day. Tonight, we're here to learn about the proposed plans for Best Life Village. I know some of you are opposed to this plan and some of you are in favor, but remember, we are here to learn and to ask questions, so at this time, I'm going to turn the meeting over to Marla Galani."

Penny stepped away from the lectern without giving Marla so much as a glance.

Marla strode forward, looking confident and comfortable in the outfit Suzanne had picked out for her—jeans, boots, and a sweatshirt. No gemstone jewelry tonight. If Marla intended to get the town's approval, she needed to look more like the people who lived here.

"Good evening." Marla paused for effect. "This time, I promise I won't collapse in front of you."

The audience tittered, then she continued. "First, I'd like to introduce the leadership team for Best Life Village." She extended her hand to the front row. "Grace, Mitch, Jesse, and Suzanne—please stand."

As the foursome stood and turned around, Marla explained their roles. "Grace will manage the community once it's built. Mitch and Jesse are overseeing all the construction, and Suzanne is our design consultant."

The crowd politely applauded.

"Now, let's talk about the plan." Marla glanced at Suzanne and signaled for her to come forward.

Suzanne got up and placed two foam board posters on large easels. She'd made the drawings ridiculously huge so even those in the back of the room would be able to see them.

Marla lifted the mic from the lectern and stood next to Suzanne. "I'm sure most of you know Suzanne Fleming, the co-owner of Creations on Main. She's an extraordinary artist, and she did these lovely, detailed drawings. Thank you, Suzanne."

Suzanne acknowledged the comment with an abbreviated bow, then she took a step to the side to give Marla the stage.

"This is a drawing of our model home," Marla said, "six hundred twenty square feet, with a front porch and a one-car attached garage."

Mumbles came from the crowd as she pointed out the details.

"The first phase of tiny homes will be craftsman-style like this one, with low-pitched gabled roofs, wood framing, and overhanging eaves. As for paint colors, Suzanne will talk about that now."

Marla handed her the microphone, and like a TV game show model, Suzanne dramatically extended her hand toward the drawing. "The ten homes in each phase will be painted in colors that will complement the environment. The exterior of this house, for example, is painted in colors you'll find on the earth—a soft fern green and a smoky gray. Other houses will be painted in shades that come from the sky—daytime blues and whites, and all the colors of daybreak and sunset too."

"So some of the houses will be yellow?" Sharon from Hair & Care called out in her caustic voice.

"Well, yes, some will be painted various shades of yellow." What could Suzanne do but tell the truth? She'd painstakingly chosen the color schemes, and now Sharon, who thought green looked fine on hair, was going to criticize these tasteful selections?

"How about the interior colors?" The question from the back of the room interrupted Suzanne's thoughts.

"The interiors will be painted in pastel shades of beige, blue, white, or gray," Suzanne replied. "Using cool colors will make the space look larger." She flipped the poster board over to reveal a display of colors. "Here are all the possibilities. The colors here on the top will be used for exteriors, and all the ones below will be interior paint colors. I think you'll agree, there's something for everyone's taste. Any other questions?"

The room remained silent, so Suzanne handed the mic back to Marla and sat down.

Rob leaned over and whispered, "Nice job, honey."

"Thanks." She appreciated the compliment, but she still found herself suddenly questioning her choices. Should she have gotten input from some of Port Mariette's influencers? It might have reduced resistance. She was kicking herself, but there was nothing she could do about it now. As Rachel would say, *it is what it is*. Suzanne crossed her legs and focused her attention on Marla talking about the features inside each tiny home.

After Marla listed them all, she stepped to the other easel. "This drawing shows how the houses will be situated along a road that meanders through wooded land. As you can see, there will be cul-de-sacs, sidewalks, and hiking trails. Here in the middle of the plan is the community room. It will have a fully equipped gym, a kitchen and dining room for parties, and several meeting rooms for activities like yoga classes, guest speakers, and clubs."

Marla took a few steps down the center aisle. "You may be wondering, who will fill these one hundred tiny homes? The answer is—maybe you! These houses will be available to any single person who would like to rent an easy-to-maintain home with low utility costs and a place where they can enjoy the benefits of community. So, the development will have a combination of young people aging out of foster care, singles, divorced people, widows, the elderly. We chose the name of this community—Best Life Village—because just like in a village, everyone who lives here will be expected to help others, whether it's a ride to a doctor's appointment, lifting a heavy package, or writing a résumé. Helping others will enable the residents to live like all of you already do here in Port Mariette—you help one another, right?

Suzanne turned her head to watch the reaction. Some people nodded or smiled, but others sat stone-faced.

Marla forged on. "That's what creates a bond and a sense of community. We hope that Best Life Village will be like living in Port Mariette, but with no steps, little maintenance, and low utility bills."

From the back of the room someone called out, "How much will the rent be?"

Marla paused, and Suzanne hoped it was because she was formulating an answer, not having a medical emergency. She watched Marla's face and body for clues. Everything looked fine.

"We haven't worked up the numbers yet," Marla said, "but even with utilities, the rent will definitely be affordable, and my foundation will cover some of the costs for those who qualify."

Others called out questions. An elderly man spoke up first. "You said these houses are for singles only. Why couldn't my wife and I rent one?"

"There's no rule against it," Marla said, "but once you tour the model home, I think you'll agree the space is too small for more than one resident."

The questions continued. Marla answered most of them herself but referred some to the rest of the team. Even Grace got to answer one.

Suzanne still couldn't tell if the majority of the people were for or against Best Life Village. She caught a look from Marla who seemed to have the same concern.

After all the questions had been answered, Penny took the mic from Marla and stepped to the lectern. "Thank you for that detailed explanation of Best Life Village." She looked over the audience. "I think the plan has some merit, but as mayor, I am concerned about an increase in crime and the harmful environmental effects of a large development in a wooded area. I'm sure many of you agree."

Penny's eyes scanned the audience, and Suzanne once again turned to see everyone's reaction. To her surprise, Herbie was glowering at Penny. Wasn't she just his Mrs. Claus? Weren't they getting back together now Mary Frances was out of the picture?

A second later, she saw Herbie get up and stomp down the aisle, shaking his head.

Penny's face turned red. "Wait," she pleaded. "I haven't finished."

'Tis the Time, 'Tis the Season

Herbie stopped in his tracks and turned around. "Okay then, finish," he hollered. He crossed his arms and stood waiting for her to continue.

Penny hesitated a moment before continuing in a halting voice. "I'm also sure many of you agree that the concerns I mentioned are outweighed by the benefits of ... of what I'm sure will become a wonderful community." Penny threw on a smile and directed it at Herbie. "I, for one, have changed my mind. I have decided to support Best Life Village."

Herbie returned to his seat while Sharon called out, "My mom says she wants a yellow one."

Penny ignored her, but Grace stood up.

It was enough of a surprise that Grace had taken a seat in the front row. And now she's speaking up? Suzanne cast a sideways look at Marla, who proudly smiled back.

Grace took the mic from Penny's hands and smiled at Sharon's elderly mother. "I'm glad to hear you'd like to rent a tiny home. I'm sure you're not the only one," Grace said with enthusiasm bordering on joy. "Anyone can apply by filling out a short application. I have some here tonight. You can also get one on the BestLifeVillage.com website. I encourage anyone who is interested to apply quickly, as I expect there will be a waiting list very soon."

Sharon hurried to the front of the room to get an application for her mother. "What a great idea." She flashed a smile at Grace, then Marla.

A few others came forward for applications, then Penny stepped toward Grace and retrieved the microphone. "Thank you, Grace." She took a deep breath and looked directly at Herbie. "As mayor," she said, "I am hereby recommending to our town council members that we support this development." She turned to the other side of the room where the representatives sat together, many of them with arms crossed.

"Are you all in agreement?" Penny asked, hand on her hip.

A few of them shrugged, some nodded, and after a few minutes of back-and-forth with Penny, every one of them agreed they'd support the plan.

"Wonderful!" she said. "How about we give the Best Life Village team a round of applause." Penny lifted her hands while keeping her eyes glued on one side of the room.

Suzanne turned around to confirm her suspicion. Yep. Penny was staring at Herbie. He was clapping enthusiastically, then he stood, and the rest of the room soon erupted into a standing ovation.

Suzanne leaned into Marla and whispered, "Thank you, Herbie." They pressed together and laughed at the strange miracle they'd just witnessed.

'Tis the Time, 'Tis the Season

Chapter 63

RACHEL

July

Rachel trailed behind Marla and Suzanne, pausing to snap photos of the first phase of tiny homes at Best Life Village. This morning's early light cast dramatic long shadows, bathing their exteriors in warm hues.

She caught up with Marla and Suzanne. "They're amazing. I love 'em all." Each one of the homes exceeded Rachel's expectations, and her eyes were wide with excitement. "Any chance we can look inside one?"

"Sure." Marla pointed to a taupe-colored home with a creamy white porch and shuttered windows. "Let's go see the model. It's fully furnished."

The three of them tiptoed over a temporary walkway of cement blocks and went inside.

Rachel entered last. Her head bobbled from left to right, then up and down. "My goodness, you've thought of everything—a fold-up dining table, lots of counter space, a stacked washer and dryer, sliding barn doors, shelves everywhere." She put her hands on her hips as she made her way around. "And with such large windows, you don't feel hemmed in."

"Having a porch helps too," Marla said. "Each home will have one, whether it's on the front, back or side. A few of them will even have a wraparound. Porches extend the usable space, at least a good part of the year."

"I love porches." Rachel cocked her head. "How many square feet is this?"

Marla glanced around, as if mentally calculating. "I think this one's about six hundred."

Rachel plopped down onto an upholstered chair. "This place is incredible." She examined the space, envisioning how she might cook, clean, relax, and sleep in such a space.

Marla pulled out an armless dining chair and took a seat. "Well, Rachel, maybe you want to apply for one of the remaining houses. What do you think?"

Suzanne raised an eyebrow. "You aren't serious about moving here, are you?"

"Yes, I am," Rachel said. "In fact, if I knew I'd never remarry, I would definitely want to live here—if dogs are allowed, that is." Cinders had been with her through thick and thin. She could never give him to anyone else, even Pete.

"Don't worry, pets are allowed." Marla smiled. "But outside, you'd have to keep Cinders on a leash."

Suzanne leaned forward. "I don't mean to pry, but don't you think at some point you and Tony might get married?"

"Eh." Rachel shrugged. "We've been talking about it off and on for months. I keep telling him I've got a lot of learning to do before I'm ready." Rachel dropped her voice to a whisper. "Besides, I'm worried about his health. He's so stressed over the mess his son has made at Signore's, and last night, he told me he's been having chest pains."

'Tis the Time,' Tis the Season

"Chest pains!" Concern was written all over Marla's face. "Did he go to the ER?"

"I tried to get him there, but he refused to go. He insisted it was just due to stress. Maybe he's right. He still drives up to Pittsburgh almost every day, trying to fix all the problems his son has caused since taking over the restaurant." What if his chest pain wasn't stress but a heart attack? Rachel couldn't imagine losing a second husband the same way.

She glanced at her phone. "He promised me he'd call a doctor today, but I haven't heard from him yet."

"It's not even eight. No one's in yet." Suzanne's voice was soothing. "I'm sure he'll call you soon."

Marla pursed her lips. "I really wish he'd go to the ER."

"He can be so stubborn," Rachel said, a note of irritation in her voice. "I can tell him what I think he should do, but that doesn't mean he's gonna do it. He'd rather try to untangle the problems at Signore's than see a doctor."

Peeved, Rachel flicked her wrist. "I wish he'd take better care of himself. Since Stan died, I've learned how to do that. After all, no one else will do it for me. That may sound like common sense, but it's a lesson I had to learn." She fell silent, concerned she may have talked too much about herself and Tony. She'd been learning not to do that too.

"Well," Marla said, "you're not the only one who's been learning a lot lately." She looked out the window. "I've realized the time I have on this earth is short. I'm trying to make the most of the time I have left."

"What caused the change in your thinking?" Rachel figured it was probably the second mini-stroke that did it. Marla had sold her Manhattan condo, and along with Grace, completely devoted herself to Best Life Village. Yet Marla seemed different on the inside too.

Marla hesitated, as if gathering her thoughts. "Landing in the hospital again certainly laid the groundwork—but it was Mitch who helped me figure things out."

"I've noticed the difference in you," Rachel said, hoping others had noticed she'd been working on herself too.

"We've all been changing," Marla said. "You've both changed too. And now," she said with a knowing smile, "I'm kind of looking forward to what lies ahead."

"You mean heaven?" Suzanne said, her eyes widened.

Rachel couldn't believe they were sitting here talking about death. Tony might be inches away from it right now. Tears formed in her eyes, but she willed them not to fall. "I don't want to think about death and dying, at least not right now," she whimpered.

"I meant the adventures lying ahead," Marla said. "Sorry it came out wrong."

Rachel's phone buzzed a text.

TONY: I'm in the ER. I'll call you when I can talk.

Chapter 64

MARLA

A Year Later, on Christmas Day

Marla had already run the vacuum, added a leaf to the dining room table, and attended an early Christmas Day service with Mitch. Since he'd shoveled the snow out front, all she had to do now was wait for Rachel and Suzanne to show up with the dinner and dessert.

Taking care not to wrinkle her black satin dress, Marla eased onto the loveseat, sinking into the soft cushion with a sigh. Lounging was something she hadn't done much of this past year, and she welcomed the moment of peace. She allowed herself to simply be, feeling the weight of the year's triumphs and challenges settle like a blanket around her shoulders.

Best Life Village had been filling up fast, putting demands on everyone on the team. Yet Marla wouldn't have it any other way. Every day, she spent time with Grace, Mitch, Suzanne, and Jesse. Rachel had joined the team, too, as the lunchtime caterer for all the workers. It saved time having meals delivered, and the crew appreciated not having to pack a lunch. Rob routinely showed up to interview new residents for his case study about youth successfully transitioning out of foster care, eager to document their stories and share them with the world.

As she relaxed on the loveseat, Marla scanned her surroundings. The Christmas tree lights glimmered softly, casting a multi-colored glow across the room. Pinecone arrangements, carefully crafted by Suzanne, centered every table. Red candles stood tall on the dining room table, waiting to be lit. Outside, fluffy snowflakes danced from a pewter sky, a ray of sunshine breaking through the clouds. It was straight out of a Christmas card—perfect, serene.

Marla's gaze fell on the copy of yesterday's *Wall Street Journal*, still folded on the coffee table. The headline read:

MANHATTAN MILLIONAIRESS TURNS TINY TOWN UPSIDE DOWN ... WITH TINY HOUSES

For probably the tenth time, she reread the story.

> A few years ago, an article in this same space about Marla Galani and her successful Gemstones Gyms led to an irresistible buyout offer. The sale enabled her to establish a foundation, which is now developing a community of tiny homes for youth transitioning out of foster care as well as widows and other singles. Twenty homes are already occupied, with eighty more being built over the next year. Rent is partially subsidized by Galani's foundation. Residents are expected to support their neighbors according to their needs, whether it's a meal for someone ill or helping a young person prepare for a job interview. Curious visitors as well as prospective residents have been drawn to this bold concept, causing the town of Port Mariette, Pennsylvania, to experience a surge of growth not seen since the heyday of the steel—

The doorbell rang, pulling Marla back to the present. She quickly set the paper aside and hurried to the door.

'Tis the Time,' Tis the Season

"Merry Christmas!" Rachel beamed, gripping an aluminum-covered pan in her mittened hands. "There's plenty more in the van." She stepped inside, the aroma of freshly baked ham wafting from the pan. "This is really hot. I'll take it into the kitchen."

Marla grabbed her coat and gloves, and she and Rachel quickly made their way down the steps.

Tony's coming a little later," Rachel said, as she pulled the van door open wide. "No way would I let him help carry these heavy pans."

"Glad he's behaving," Marla said with a grin, as she reached into the van. "Open heart surgery has a long recovery time."

"You're not kidding," Rachel said. "They told him a full year. That's crazy."

As the women made trips back and forth, Suzanne arrived. "Rob's coming at three," she said, a pie in hand as she stepped out of the car. "He's spending some time on the phone with both his kids."

Together, the three unloaded the meals and desserts, then organized everything in the kitchen.

"Why don't we take a break before everyone else gets here?" Marla said, popping open a bottle of sparkling cider and pouring three flutes. "Merry Christmas! Here's to a bright new year." She clinked her glass against Suzanne's and Rachel's, feeling the familiar warmth of their friendship.

"And here's to the first twenty homes now occupied at Best Life Village," Suzanne added, her eyes sparkling with pride.

Rachel clinked the glasses again. "We can't forget our new grandkids! Here's to my new granddaughter, Zoey, and to Suzanne's new grandson, Nathan."

"Here's to our very special friendship," Marla said, her voice catching.

"Through thick and thin," Suzanne added, and they all rolled their eyes and laughed, the sound filling the room with a joyful echo.

The doorbell rang again. Three o'clock on the dot. They'd been too busy giving toasts to notice the time.

"I'll get it," Marla said, scooting to the door. Mitch was already there, holding it open for Aunt Adele and Suzanne's mom. They entered, bringing with them a wave of warmth and affection. A round of hugs and kisses ensued.

Grace and Jesse arrived next, their faces lit with holiday cheer. "Merry Christmas, Mom," Grace said, wrapping Marla in a warm embrace.

Mom. The word hung in the air, sweet and tender, making Marla's heart swell with emotion.

"Merry Christmas, Daughter," she replied, her voice thick with emotion. Their eyes connected, and in that moment, Marla knew that all the heartache and struggle had been worth it.

The bell soon rang again, and Jill, Drew, Elizabeth, and baby Nathan came inside, bringing more warmth, more love.

"He's as precious as baby Jesus," Suzanne whispered as she reached for her grandson. "So innocent."

As Jill and Drew were taking off their coats, Rob and Tony showed up, palling around like old friends.

Pete arrived last, holding Lindsey's hand on one side and clutching a carrier with the other. Baby Zoey was sound asleep, her tiny chest rising and falling in peaceful slumber.

Rachel kissed her fingertips then touched the sleeping baby's cheek. Marla took their coats. "Maybe someday Zoey and Nathan will get married," Rachel said to Suzanne, giggling.

'Tis the Time,' Tis the Season

Tony handed Marla his jacket, a grin wide across his face. "Everything smells great."

She gently elbowed his arm. "You know you can thank Rachel for that."

"Where do you want us to sit, Mom?" Grace asked, standing near the end of the long table.

Marla's breath caught in her throat. It wasn't a fluke—Grace was really calling her Mom now. The word wrapped around her heart, warming her all over. She walked alongside the table, smiling as she pointed out the seating assignments, her heart nearly bursting with happiness.

Once everyone had settled in, Marla, Rachel, and Suzanne served the meals. Seventeen people filled the room with noise and laughter, peppered with the sound of forks clinking against plates and babies cooing.

Every person Marla loved sat at this table. Her eyes misty, she wished the day would never end. How different her life would have been if Suzanne and Rachel hadn't opened their arms to her all those years ago. Their act of kindness had led to so much joy for so many people. Where would she be now if those two hadn't intervened in her life? She had no idea how much time she had left on this earth, but one thing she knew for sure—God had blessed her with a good life. He'd also blessed her with wealth, and in turn, she could bless others. His plan was all so clear now.

Without Suzanne and Rachel, she never would have met Mitch either. Working with him on Best Life Village, they'd grown even closer. Every day was a new challenge to overcome, and together, they tackled each one with a spirit of determination and faith. Mitch never complained, even though he had to draw up plans, acquire permits, arrange for utilities, and clear the land—on top of overseeing all the construction. He'd rounded up every man who'd ever worked for him and hired plenty of apprentices too—young talent from August Village, all of them trained under Jesse's watchful eye.

With such a large crew, the first two phases of the community—twenty homes—were already completed and occupied. The community thrived, a testament to what could be achieved when people came together with a shared purpose.

Grace was in charge of applications from youth aging out of foster care, and Marla handled applications from seniors and other singles. The mix of ages enabled residents to help one another in all sorts of ways. Isaiah and Landon had used a grant from Marla's foundation to buy a van for a shuttle business, and riders sometimes bartered for rides. Sharon's mom always offered to cut her driver's hair. Others helped neighbors with computer problems, balancing a checkbook, or even opening a jar.

Suzanne's color schemes and exterior designs had turned these tiny houses into artistic gems. The craftsman style homes in the first phase blended well with the wooded landscape, and the sleek lines and big windows of the contemporary homes in the second phase had an appeal of their own. The eight remaining phases would feature a range of architectural styles—gingerbread, southern shotgun, rustic, and others. Mixed together, this community of one hundred tiny houses was creating a fascinating place to live, and like a magnet, it was drawing more and more visitors to Port Mariette to live, work, and shop.

Rob had recommended every tiny home have a front porch. It would foster a sense of community, he said. Rob also volunteered to work with residents on identifying ways to use their unique skills and life experiences to help others within Best Life Village and beyond.

All these efforts strengthened the sense of community, and Marla couldn't help but feel a deep sense of pride and gratitude. Her heart swelled as she looked around the room, taking in everyone's faces. This was the family she had always dreamed of but never thought possible.

Mitch caught her gaze from across the table, his eyes reflecting the same profound happiness she felt. The meal now over, he made his way to her side while she rose from her chair. He wrapped an arm around her waist and led her to the Christmas tree, where the lights cast a kaleidoscope of colors across their faces.

"Quite the gathering you've orchestrated." Mitch's voice was filled with admiration, as the others joined them in the living room. He took both her hands in his, his thumbs gently caressing her skin.

Marla felt her heartbeat quicken.

The room suddenly grew quiet as all eyes turned toward them, sensing something special was about to happen.

"Marla," he began, his voice steady but filled with emotion, "the past year has been the most incredible journey. Working alongside you, building this community, and sharing time with you and everyone here today has taught me about love in its purest form."

He reached into his pocket and pulled out a small velvet box. Marla's breath caught as he lowered himself onto one knee. The room erupted into soft gasps and whispered excitement. Tears suddenly pooled in Marla's eyes, and her hands trembled slightly.

"Marla Galani, you have transformed my world and the worlds of so many others. I can't imagine my life without you in it. Will you do me the honor of becoming my wife and continuing this beautiful journey together?" Mitch opened the box to reveal a stunning diamond ring that sparkled brilliantly next to the tree lights.

For a moment, time seemed to stand still. Marla felt a wave of emotions crash over her—joy, love, gratitude, and a profound sense of belonging. Tears ran down her cheeks and her voice quivered as she attempted to reply.

"Oh, Mitch, oh my!"

"Is that your answer?" Mitch teased, his eyes smiling.

"My answer?" She stretched out her left hand, allowing Mitch to slide the ring onto her finger. "Yes, Mitch. Yes! A thousand times, yes!"

Author Note

Dear Readers,

Thank you for reading *'Tis the Time, 'Tis the Season*, the third book in the *Next Act* trilogy. I hope you related to these women as they continued to grow and change, and their stories encouraged and inspired you.

If you are a member of a book club, library, church, or organization seeking speakers, I'd be delighted to speak to your group in person or online about any aspect of fiction and nonfiction writing. As a former talk radio host, I enjoy speaking as much as writing! My email is chris@chrisposti.com and I'd love to hear from you.

PS—Sign up for my newsletters at https://chrisposti.com/, and I'll send you something surprising.

PPS—If you enjoyed the book, would you please take two minutes to write a brief review on Amazon? It would mean so much. Thank you!

About the Author

Chris Posti is a longtime newspaper columnist as well as a career and executive coach. After writing three nonfiction books, she turned to writing novels when she realized how few novels feature women over fifty as their main characters.

Chris lives with her husband in a suburb south of Pittsburgh, Pennsylvania. If she's not writing, she's probably playing with her grandsons, creating something artsy, or helping to organize her next high school reunion.

Questions for Discussion

1. Which characters did you identify with the most (or least), and why?

2. Friendship is one of the themes of this story. Have you ever experienced the loss of a longtime friendship, or even a recent one? Do you know why it happened? Is it a friendship you can attempt to resurrect? How might you do that?

3. If you were suddenly blessed with wealth like Marla, what would you do with all that money? Does your current style of spending reflect the values you believe you hold dear?

4. Rachel takes on the presidency of PMBA, a role which is just outside her comfort zone. Have you ever stretched yourself in a new role? How did it change you?

5. Suzanne has difficulty understanding her daughter, Jill, and son-in-law, Drew. Why do you suppose she struggles so much? What could she do to improve the situation?

6. Although Marla's religious background was limited, she still realized she had broken one of the Ten Commandments when she lied. She probably would not have been able to recite all ten. Can you?

7. Suzanne's memories of the poor box affected her throughout her life. What experiences did you have as a child that profoundly influenced your thinking or behavior as an adult?

8. Mitch was taken with Marla the moment he met her, but he didn't make a move for a long time. Was it because Warren was in the picture, or were there other reasons?

9. Imagine living in a tiny house. How would your life be different?

10. Grace gave Marla quite the education about foster care and youth aging out of the system. Was it an eye-opener for you too? How might this knowledge influence your future behavior? If you have experience with foster care, what else would you like people to know or do?

The Sinner's Prayer

The Sinner's Prayer is a verbal commitment to God, said when a person is ready to repent of their sins, ask God for forgiveness, and state their belief in the life, death, and resurrection of Jesus Christ. The Bible tells us that "if you declare with your mouth, 'Jesus is Lord,' and believe in your heart that God raised him from the dead, you will be saved. For it is with your heart that you believe and are justified, and it is with your mouth that you profess your faith and are saved." (Romans 10:9-10 NIV).

The specific words of the prayer can greatly vary. What matters is the repentance and the faith of the person saying the prayer. Here's an example of what you might say:

> Dear God, I know I am a sinner. I am sorry for all the sins I have committed and I ask for your forgiveness. Lord Jesus, I believe you died to pay the price for my sins and that you rose from the dead. By faith I receive you into my heart as my Lord and Savior. From this moment on, help me to live for only you. In Jesus's name I pray. Amen.

If you said that prayer and truly meant it, God will help you change. Now, start reading the Bible, pray regularly, tell others about your decision to follow Christ, and connect with other believers at church. Once you take these steps, your life will never be the same—in fact, it will become a glorious and fascinating adventure!

Other Books in the Next Act Series

Made in the USA
Middletown, DE
07 October 2024